AWAKENED

Part II of The Sinking Man Series

By Justin S. Leslie

Copyediting - Happily Ever Proofreading

Paperback ISBN: 978-1-7353035-5-0
eBook ISBN: 978-1-7353035-4-3

Contact Information

email: Abaddonbooks@hotmail.com

Facebook: @Maxabaddonbooks Facebook Justin Leslie

Website: www.JustinLeslie.com

"It is a mistake to try to look too far ahead. The chain of destiny can only be grasped one link at a time."

WINSTON CHURCHILL

CHAPTER 1

"**W**ell, well, well," Ben said, handing the binoculars to Ian.

The two men were finally making their way to the battery shop after an unforeseen holdup when part of the road before reaching the Julington Creek bridge had flooded, forcing a three-week delay.

Ben had learned that things would more than likely go wrong every time one left the secluded neighborhood's safety, or at least go slightly sideways. Getting to the battery store had still been a priority, though, and one that Kelly, Ian, and Ben would not let sit idle.

"That's it for sure," Ian agreed, referring to the red truck they had ran into previously.

They were two streetlights—Ben measured distance on San Jose Boulevard by the streetlights—away from their final destination: the battery store. It was the same red truck that had been at the gas station north of the I-295 overpass. The person driving that vehicle was seemingly shadowing them. At least that's what they thought.

Ian handed Ben the binoculars as they continued to scan the small mini-mart. Whoever was driving was again stopping at a gas station.

"Hold on, there he is," Ben drawled under his breath, handing over the binoculars.

"Dammit," Ian whispered. "That's him."

"Who?" Ben asked.

"The guy we saw at the Veterans Arena. I'm sure. The guy's built like a tank. You don't see too many folks like that around, present company excluded," Ian said, clicking the radio on his vest.

Ian and Kelly had gone to the Brinkman's house and found the rest of the radio kits in another box, which included earpieces and communicators that clipped on one's shoulder like cops would wear, the cable's curly tail snaking through the vest.

"Red-Hot One, over," Ian said. They had given each other radio call signs, and that one meant Kelly.

"Go ahead," she replied. She had obviously been standing by the radio.

"You're not going to believe this. That guy from the Arena? Well, he is the person that was driving the red truck, and he's across the street getting what looks like beer from another gas station," Ian rattled off.

The two of them were currently on top of the one-story shopping center across the street, concealed by trees and shade. The building was intact. People hadn't been interested in looting barbershops or restaurants when things had taken a turn for the worse.

Ben had insisted on checking out a couple of side roads, also not forgetting about the zombies' habit of lingering in the shadows, staying out of the sun. As luck would have it, he had taken the truck down a side street, driving along a back road leading them to find the mysterious red truck.

Ben looked down at his watch as Eve vibrated, noting it was noon, time for lunch. He had gotten better at switching her to vibrate.

Eve was the latest in smartwatch technology. Programmable and, after an initial setup, not reliant on the Internet to operate. It learned and adapted to its owner. As long as you had a working computer, you could do just about anything with one.

"What's the plan?" Ian asked as Ben continued watching.

"Let's see if this is our radio guy," he replied, grabbing his radio, switching over to the channel with the clicking. The two men waited for the lumbering man to walk back out. After a handful of minutes, he again made his way to the truck with an armful of supplies. He had a hood over his head and sunglasses, making it hard to see his face.

"Hey," Ben said over the radio, causing the man to pause. After setting down the box he was carrying, the man pulled the radio from his vest clip.

"Why isn't he responding?" Ian asked as Ben chuckled lightly.

"He probably just thinks we're the people we made up on the radios. Doesn't know we are talking to him." Ben's statement was correct, as the man didn't even bother scanning the area. He instead chose to focus on the radio. The man put it up to his ear, actuating the button and proving it was him on the other end sending out the clicks.

Ben looked at Ian as he returned the clicks. Much to Ben's surprise, the man lost interest in the radio after a handful of seconds, pushing his newly acquired loot further into the bed of his truck.

"That's weird as shit. He got all excited, then just went back to it," Ian said in a hushed tone.

Ben nodded, figuring it was time to act. Either way, they would more than likely run into the man to get to their planned destination. Ben would rather have the upper hand. After all, there were two of them to one of whoever that was.

"Hey, my name's Ben. I'm going to ask this once. Set the box down, put your radio in your right hand, and hold up your other one," Ben said, getting the man's full attention. Thinking on the fly, he handed the radio to Ian. The mysterious person would hear two voices, making him believe he could be surrounded.

"Slowly walk out into the street. If you have a weapon, nod your head," Ian added, handing the radio back to Ben. Ian's youth showed as he snickered under his breath.

The man obliged, nodding his head in affirmation, walking out to the edge of the road. Not far enough to be out of range of his truck, but enough for the two of them to see around him.

"Alright, I'm not going to ask you to do any more than we already have. We know you have a weapon, and you can keep that," Ben said, hoping it may build some trust.

The man nodded his head slightly in a confused manner, but the tactic had worked. Taking a deep breath, the tension dissolved from his body. The mysterious man figured he was either about to die and it didn't matter, or he would at least be able to reason with the group surrounding him.

Ben clicked off the radio. "What do we do?" Ian asked him as Ben started shuffling backward toward the ladder.

As the two men dropped to the ground, Ben hesitated. He scanned the trees behind the building.

"You hear something?" Ian asked, pulling up his rifle.

"I don't think so. Let's play this safe. Go back to the truck and pull it up to the intersection. Once you're in and moving, I'll walk out. That will make it look like we are spread out. Once you get out, we will go have a little chat," Ben instructed, motioning that he would walk around the other side of the building.

"You think he's still there?"

"Yeah, I'm pretty sure we spooked him," Ben confirmed before Ian jogged off to the truck.

While not much time had passed since he had first ventured out of his private paradise, Ben had learned several lessons in quick succession about sticking close to wooded areas. Zombies didn't like the sun and preferred to linger in the shadows. He looked back at the tree line again, thinking he'd heard a noise.

Shaking it off, Ben walked around the far end of the one-story shopping center, getting a clear view of the man still standing in the open. The sound of the truck pulling silently into the intersection came as Ben walked out. Taking Ian and Kelly's advice, he kept his weapon lowered. Moving forward, he put his hands palm up as the trusty Toyota Tacoma stopped on the other side of the man.

"Name's Ben. We've noticed you around lately and think it's a good time for a chat," he said as the man pulled the hood back off his head. He was in his early forties, with light gray peppering his hair. What was immediately evident to Ben and Ian was the strength behind his gaze and size. While not as large as Ben, it was clear this person was strong. He wore what looked like a tool belt full of odd trinkets. These included a rather used-looking claw hammer, two pistols, and a machete.

"Dan, my name's Dan," the man said in a regular cadence. If he was nervous, he wasn't showing it.

"Alright, Dan, I'm sure you understand about us being cautious. My friend Ian has a few things he wants to ask you about," Ben said, referring to Ian getting clarification on the messed-up scene at the Veterans Arena. There was no doubt in Ian's mind this was the person they had witnessed taking someone bound in chains. Kelly and Ian had spent quite some time their first night staying in Ben's house, discussing what may have happened to the poor soul.

Ben and Ian had not planned on running into anyone for certain. They had, however, discussed the strange man and what they would do if another encounter occurred. Like most plans, the one they'd made to stay distant had been thrown out the window. Dan was too close and getting closer to their hidden paradise.

Ben nodded at Ian.

"What was up with the person you had shackled at the Veterans Arena?" he asked.

A stunned expression solidified on Dan's face. The man was startled by not only the two of them taking him by surprise but by the knowledge that they may have been tracking him. As soon as Dan started worrying, he quickly let the stiffness out of his body. That wasn't a person; it was a zombie, or close to being one.

Dan chuckled. "You mean that bag of bones that tried to eat me? It was a crazy. Not fully turned."

Ian cocked his head, looking at Ben for guidance.

"How long have you been at the Arena?" Ben asked.

"A few weeks. I picked up a signal and went to check it out. The place was swarming. I started clearing it out, then started getting all these people showing up on the radio. You know Tina and Jimmy?" Dan asked, assuming Ben was in charge, slightly turning his back toward Ian.

Ian chuckled lightly. Ben didn't, however. "How did you know where those radio signals were coming from?" He figured there was more to Dan than initial appearances suggested.

"I can show you. Mind if I grab something out of my truck and have a smoke?"

Ben nodded. Dan reached down into the breast pocket of his shirt, pulling out a pack of cigarettes, lighting one up. His shirt looked like a military uniform of sorts, the type you could get from an Army-Navy store. The type people called official, when in reality, it was used for paintball or by hunters. He took a long drag, letting a roll of smoke billow from his hungry lungs.

"I'm all about trust here. Move slowly, and I'll walk over," Ben said as Dan just shrugged.

Ben positioned himself behind Dan as the man ruffled through a bag in the passenger seat. Before Ben or Ian could react, he pulled up a rifle, pointing it directly at Ben, who dove forward out of the way of the barrel as several rounds barked from the assault rifle. *Tacka, tacka, tacka,* rang in Ben's ears.

Ian swung around, sighting in on Dan as several more rounds exploded from the truck. He couldn't tell if Dan was trying to shoot Ben or swing around to him. Then he saw it. A wall of zombies erupting from the building and tree line the two had just left. Dan was cutting through the group with laser-like precision, the cigarette still hanging from his mouth.

Ben rolled around, the initial shock of still having a head wearing off. Then he saw it. Dan had more than likely saved their lives, or at least given them a running start. After another slight pause, Ben pulled up his own rifle, firing several more rounds into the legs of the closest zombies, forcing a few others to trip, and slowing them down.

Ian, by then, had joined the party. His rounds sounded different, reverberating loudly as small explosions took chunks out of the group, spraying gore on the pavement.

The three men circled the red truck as they continued to mow down the thinning group. These were slow zombies. Old, and by the looks of it, twenty to thirty rows deep of the lumbering figures.

After another minute, the group of zombies was nothing more than a pile of gore and broken bodies. The smell of gunpowder filled the air, as well as a light smokey haze. Dan held his hand up in a fist, the universal signal to stop. Ian and Ben looked at each other as Dan offered them his pack of cigarettes; they just shook their heads. Everyone's ears were ringing.

"More for me," Dan said. His words sounded muffled to the others, like being underwater.

CHAPTER 2

The three men stood inside the convenience store, avoiding the stench of the corpses lying outside.

Dan handed Ben a high-end RF detector. "So I started following the signals," Dan said, explaining what had directed him south.

The device was one Ben was not familiar with. It had several knobs and a screen that looked to be directional. Meaning, if one were talking on the radio, the screen would produce an arrow, the brightness increasing as one came closer to the other signal.

The little skits Ian and Kelly had been putting on, followed by my clicks, had directed Dan in our general direction.

After another minute of Ben looking at the device, Dan interjected. "Got it from a search and rescue company. That's where I got most of my gear. The place was a gold mine. Looking for police stations, armories, or survival stores is good and all, but I'm telling you, this place had them all beat. Plus, I think the one here was up to some shady stuff."

Ian chuckled lightly, still nervous about the man. "So you would have stayed put if we hadn't jumped on these radios."

"Yup," Dan confirmed, cracking the top off a beer.

Ben regarded the man as he handed him the bottle. "Day drinking is in my list of approved rules," Ben mumbled.

"Cheers! To new friends," Dan said before the two men took pulls from their warm beers. It was clear Dan was used to having the stuff at room temperature. Ben gagged momentarily before taking another sip.

"So, now that's out of the way, what's your story?" Ian asked before Ben could.

Dan looked at the young man as Ben added, "Look, this isn't our turf or whatever they call it these days. It's like our backyard, so to speak. We don't see many if any people down here." He was making it seem as if he had been out with his newfound friends Ian and Kelly frequently. Ben wasn't trying to deceive Dan, just get an understanding of his intentions.

"Well, I'm here looking for a friend of mine and to see if taking I-95 is a viable option. My better half is waiting for me to get back. After hearing the radio signals, I figured I'd stick around a few more days and check it out," Dan said, lighting another smoke off the one he was finishing.

Dan went on to explain how his friend Dustin had been stuck on the base, being part of some military operation when the others left. Dustin's wife, Tina; his wife, Shelly; and Dan had made their way west toward Tallahassee, only to end up leaving the city.

That piqued Ben's interest. Dan had been close to the very place his wife, Sarah, was more than likely at.

"We never heard anyone else talking," Ian said, referring to the radio scans Kelly had done previously.

"Not all those clicks were me," Dan replied grinning. "Be careful what you say in those. We learned that lesson."

"Tell me about the panhandle," Ben requested, still focused on Sarah. He would figure out how to handle this new visitor later. Ben was also concerned that if Dan was getting close to finding them, so might others. Then he thought about the chances, slightly relaxing. This man was a one-off. He concluded that the group would work out a system when using the radios.

"We had gone to Steinhatchee to stay at an old summer rental a friend of ours owned. It was tucked away, and we all knew about it. Dustin told us to stay put till he returned. He was in the army," Dan paused, looking at me. He was sizing me up, guessing the same. Jacksonville was a large military town, with all branches of the armed forces represented. Even the Coast Guard.

"After four months, we figured he might not be coming back. You know, gone. Long story short, we decided to head back to Jacksonville to find him. Ended up running into some people that told us about the bombing," Dan said, flicking his cigarette onto the ground, letting it smolder.

"So, where is the rest of your people? In Tallahassee? Seems out of the way," Ben asked, wanting to get to the point.

"Ah, yes, after hearing that, the group we ran into told us about Tallahassee, so we picked up and headed that way. It would give the girls a place to stay while I checked out Jacksonville. Where did you say you're from again?" The adrenaline from the fight was washing out of his system, bringing him into focus again. He had been talking and giving up a good amount of information.

Ian spoke, "Close, that's why we're asking. We haven't been west."

The young man came across as genuine. He was, and Dan could see that. Ben, on the other hand, was an anomaly he would have to figure out. He sighed. "There is a community there. It's large. Everything seemed great at first, and then it got complicated."

"What do you mean by complicated?" Ben asked, hearing that word for the second time recently. Sarah, his wife, had said things had gotten complicated. He didn't like that word.

"Not bad, just weird. They're doing good things there, just . . . Let's put it this way. The world as we know it is over. You know, for those still alive, the world is literally your oyster. They wanted us to work, and when they wanted to assign us to stay in a certain building, we decided it was time to go. It was just a little too stiff for our taste," Dan explained as Eve chirped to life on Ben's wrist. He had turned the volume back on while Dan was talking.

"You should now be at your destination. Are you on schedule?" the programmed female's voice of Ben's smartwatch, Eve, chirped.

"Push back alarms two hours," Ben instructed, getting more comfortable with talking to Eve in front of people.

Dan looked at the watch with focused curiosity. He picked up that the two men had a place to be at a certain time. In reality, Ben just kept up with the time and treated trips outside the walls of his paradise as if they were a military operation. Getting caught out after dark was not an option, not to mention Ben was still not fully used to being around others, as only a few short weeks had passed. Eve brought him a feeling of comfort and connection to home.

The crazies and zombies came out in the night mist, for some reason avoiding the sun during the day.

"Did you meet anyone named Sarah? She's a doctor," Ben asked, throwing it out there.

Ben figured since Sarah was in Florida, that she was more than likely at the same place. Per her message, she was, in fact, in Tallahassee. It would be another week or so before the phones would work simultaneously per his calculation, the phone's inscription keys slipping more and more as the days went by.

Dan thought about it for a minute. He raised his hand, scratching his beard. An anchor tattoo peeked out from under his sleeve; the man had been in the Navy at some point, Ben was sure of that. After witnessing the carnage he'd unleashed on the zombies, Ben had been focusing on the man, looking at slight details and nuances to see if there was anything off.

"Blonde lady, shorter, a looker for sure, came from out west somewhere. Denver, I think," Dan said as Ben's heart raced.

"Your heart rate is elevated. How about some Coldplay to calm you down?" Eve suggested before Ben could stop her.

"Haha, you like Coldplay." Ian snickered, taking a jab at the music. Ben looked over, shaking his head.

"What did she say? Do? Tell me everything," Ben requested.

Dan told him all he knew, which wasn't much. She was a doctor, and more importantly, very high profile. She stayed in a place called the tower and had her own security, or as Dan called them, handlers.

After exhausting all of the details, Ian chimed back in.

"Tell us about your wife?" he said, getting a toothy grin out of Dan. Ben, on the other hand, was not listening; he was calculating. The word "complicated" swam through his mind.

Is she being kept there? Handlers? Ben thought.

Dan went on to explain that his and Dustin's wives were staying off I-10, on a farm close to Interstate 75. They had simply wandered out of the community. From there, his details became vague. He, same as Ben, wanted to keep the rest close to his chest. The one thing he was sure of was that his friend Dustin was still alive. This was based on a report from another person that had shown up in Tallahassee. If found, they would return to the women, and they planned on heading south.

"South?" Ben asked, snapping out of his thoughts quizzically.

"Yup," was all Dan said.

Ben looked at Ian.

"You know anything about the conditions down there?" Ian asked. "From what we can tell, a lot of these damn things keep going in that direction. That is, if they don't get caught up by the water or turn."

"No, we have a plan, and either way, we believe things will work out," Dan said, also looking at his watch.

Ben let out a breath, still computing everything he had just heard. It was still a little over a week till the signals from the sat phones would work.

Thoughts of adding more people to Ben's private paradise crossed his mind. While there were plenty of houses, supplies, and support for that many people could prove to be an issue, not to mention they didn't plan on staying around, which brought up another round of issues: what if they told someone else? Ben didn't even know Ian and Kelly's true intentions, though he had grown to trust them in a very short amount of time.

"Okay, we have a run to make. Just go to channel 94.3 if you want to talk. We will monitor it," Ben indicated as Ian nodded, seeing Dan's reluctance. Ben continued, "If you're still around, let's plan on meeting back here in one week."

Dan looked at Ben, slight disappointment crossing his face. He wanted to go back with them. "Alright. If something comes up, I'll let you know. You do the same?" Dan asked, deciding to also see where things would go.

"Yeah," Ben agreed, holding out his hand. The three men said their goodbyes, and Ben and Ian watched Dan drive north.

CHAPTER 3

"Y ou think we can trust him?" Ian wondered as the two pulled into the front parking lot of the battery store. "It's not him I'm worried about. He knows a lot of other people, though. That story about his group sneaking out just seemed out of place, but it confirms what I needed to know. If Sarah can't sneak out, as he put it, I'm going to have to go get her," Ben concluded, turning off the truck and staring at the empty shop front.

"You think he can find us with that meter he had?" Ian followed up, asking the same question Ben was asking himself.

Ben pulled out a full bottle of rum, taking a long sip, wincing at the tail end. He had found himself hitting the booze more than before, which was already a good amount.

"Yup. When we get back, we will go over some new rules for the radios. As long as we aren't transmitting, he can't locate us. The thing will get him close, and with the water on one side, it will make it even easier. Only one direction to go. I don't think he had figured it out yet, plus the road was flooded," Ben said, handing the bottle to Ian.

"You need to relax with this stuff in the morning," Ian said, taking his own much less substantial pull.

"Pot . . . kettle . . . black, young man. Plus, day drinking is in the list of approved rules," Ben said as the two chuckled. He had kept up with his little game of making odd rules. Kelly and Ian had even joined him.

"What's the plan?" Ian asked as Ben opened the door, grabbing his rifle. The death machine smelled of carbon from its recent use.

"We go in, get what we need, and get back. Today's already gone off the rails once; I'd like to keep that to a minimum. Plus, I'd like to get that zone back up and running. That way, we can turn the rest of the systems on and possibly get some power to another house. Going to check out the boats like we mentioned will have to wait," Ben said as Ian nodded. Before leaving, the group had decided on acquiring a boat to travel up and down the river. Ben was still on edge, considering the body that had washed up in the inlet several weeks ago.

The two men did a coordinated sweep of the area. Kelly and Ian had taken some time to show Ben their tactics while out and about. Ben's ego took a back seat for once as he learned from his two younger companions.

"Clear?" Ben asked. Ian replied with the same. The two of them walked to the front of the shop.

The good thing about the store was that it was close to the main road and had an entire parking lot behind it. The area would make any zombies in the area have to cross a large swath of open space, making it easier to see. While riddled with cars, it would still be nearly impossible for a larger group to get the drop on them as they had earlier.

Ben rapped the glass, waiting for any reaction. None came. While freestanding, the store had two other shops attached: a cell phone store with a busted front window and a small coffee shop. Ben shook his head.

"Dumbshits. The world's ending, and everyone wants to get their phone upgraded."

Ian nodded.

Walking up, Ian pulled out a hammer, smashing the section of filthy glass from around the locked door. It was clear zombies had been through here rubbing against the windows. The hammer bounced back as security bars prevented him from breaking all the way through.

Ian grabbed his wrist, bending over, cursing under his breath. "Dammit."

"You okay?" Ben asked, walking up to inspect the obstacle. He now understood why the store hadn't been looted. It would have been clear once upon a time when the windows were clean that the shop was secured.

"Fine, just a little stinger," Ian said, walking back to the truck.

"Bolt cutters?" Ben asked as he pulled his flask out, taking a pull. It helped him think and calmed his nerves.

Ian didn't reply as he continued to grumble under his breath. The day had so far been a compost of errors. Dan, the zombies, the gate. The two men separately had the same feeling that the world, in general, was fucking with them.

Ian returned with the bolt cutter, a must-have when out in the road. The sound of breaking glass coming from the sea of cars caught their attention.

"I think it's a stray, maybe an animal," Ben said after a moment's pause. "Let's get moving. I've got an idea. Let's keep this storefront intact and see if we can get in from the rear of the building."

Ian agreed, and the two men headed towards the rear of the building. As noted before, the building was in the parking lot of a large package store—Walmart, to be precise—and was open on all sides, giving the two men more comfort in their ability to react if needed.

In the back of Ben's mind was Dan; while betting the man had in fact gone back north, he had the feeling they were being watched.

The back door was locked; however, it seemed to be a much easier point of entrance compared to cutting through bars and the cage on the front doors. Only a thick chain around a padlock pushed into a cover secured the door.

"I bet whoever worked here planned on coming back and didn't want their shit taken. This place is a gold mine," Ben said, grinning as Ian made quick work of the locks, the metal clanking off the concrete.

"I noticed the sign wasn't up, like they took it down," Ian noted.

"They did. Let's get moving," Ben said as the door opened.

Eve decided to join the conversation. "You have completed four thousand steps today. Keep it up. You have four hundred new alerts."

Ben froze. "New alerts?"

Ian, not knowing why this was important, paused to look around the parking lot before opening the door.

"What the hell . . ." Ben trailed off. He shook his head, clicking the watch off as Ian slowly opened the door. A muffled alarm started ringing from inside the room. The building either had power or the system was running off solar batteries like Ben's.

They knew they didn't have much time to find the source and shut it off before drawing more attention than they already had. The two had already made plenty of commotion a few miles south when they'd met Dan, but here the noise was piercing, and it carried.

"Dammit," Ian barked, looking wildly around and cursing as Ben finally found the source of the earsplitting noise. He pulled out the big ass Rambo knife he had snuggly attached to his vest. Slashing above the door, the alarm immediately stopped ringing like a dinner bell dropping to the floor.

"Look," Ian said, pointing to the wires coming out of the wall. "Power."

Ben looked down at the switch on the wall, having to put a lot of effort into turning it on. LED track lights sprang to life in the small single-story warehouse. The room was roughly one thousand square feet with a small office walled off in the corner. The front sales room was on the other side of a door with a two-way glass. Squinting, Ben could see the front door.

"Bet those looters were sure glad they got their new big-screen TVs and skipped this place," Ben said sarcastically. He liked making fun of the random stores that had been looted, or what had been taken to help with the end of the world. In most instances, large TV boxes lay strewn in front of the box stores. It seemed to be the item of the apocalypse.

It just reminded Ben how oblivious the general population was.

"Check these out," Ian said, pointing to several shelves stacked with solar panels.

"Looks like Christmas is coming early. I'd say there are enough here to run a small house." Ben replied, honing in on a window inside the warehouse. "Bingo . . ." Ben drawled out, heading over to the far end by the office. Sitting there were stacks of batteries just like the ones he had at the house.

"That must be more than enough," Ian said, getting excited, laying claim on the prize without asking.

"Yup. This place must have been a wholesaler. I'd even bet the guys that installed our system worked out of here," Ben deduced, seeing more of the same type of equipment.

With that knowledge, he walked into the office.

"What are you looking for?"

Ben walked back out of the office with a stack of papers. "Well, I'm thinking not only can we grab this haul in a few trips, but we can also map out the houses or locations where they installed sets like mine and this one here."

The logic was sound. Ian was impressed by Ben's ability to think on his feet; this could be a game-changer. They could even get the other houses online.

"So this could be one of our stopping points. We stock it and secure it," Ian said, getting the point. Ben nodded, stashing the papers into his backpack.

"Let's check the rest of this place out, grab the batteries we need, and get the hell out of here before zombies start showing up. I bet some are making their way through that parking lot already."

With that, the two men went to work stacking their new-found treasure by the front door. They would need a trailer to get the other ones, so for now, they loaded up as much as they could.

Ben jingled the keys to the front door he had found in the office. The gated door screeched to life as he pushed it open.

"You hear that?" Ian said, running a battery to the truck.

"Let's keep moving. I don't plan on coming back for a few days. I'm going to lock and block the back door," Ben said, jingling the keys again in front of Ian.

The two made quick work of loading the rest of the batteries. They also grabbed a few extra things. Items such as regular batteries, a few portable solar panels, and a Bluetooth speaker caught the men's attention.

Several loud thumps reverberated through the warehouse. Someone . . . something was at the back door. The thumps multiplied as Ben looked over at Ian.

"Time to go. We got more than anticipated. We'll be back," Ben said as he locked the door, thinking about their find. If he was right, they would be able to find other houses just like his, and maybe like-minded people.

Ian walked around the side of the building, getting a clear view of the parking lot. It was moving. The tops of zombie heads flowed through the wreckage of cars, giving the parking lot the look of flowing water.

"We gotta go," Ian said flatly, not letting his voice carry.

They quickly got in the truck, slowly pulling out of the parking lot, picking up speed as they hit the main road heading back south.

"Should we radio Kelly?" Ian asked, still thinking about Dan as well as the bounty they had just found.

"No. I'm not sold on Dan or what he's doing. Probably should have taken that locator or whatever it is," Ben said, looking out the window. He drove around the freshly dropped bodies in the road as they passed the gas station.

"Something's been bugging me. Where the hell do zombie bodies go? I noticed that when I first came out," Ben said, thinking there would be more. He had seen bones while dropping the radios off at the bridges, but nothing to account for the total amount of zombies out there.

"Animals, mostly. We noticed on the beach that people just left their animals. Cats, dogs, and about everything else you can imagine. Some asshats had a pet tiger that caused us an issue a few months back," Ian replied distractedly. He was preoccupied with their find, looking at the papers Ben had acquired and noting the addresses.

"See, that's the thing. Animals figured it out. Survival of the fittest. I wonder when other folks out there will do the same," Ben stated, the point that was starting to worry him about Sarah's current situation.

"Well, we think there's more than enough supplies out there. Kelly seems to think people are probably starting to figure out how to survive. At least those that have made it this far," Ian trailed off, staring out the window.

"Fingers crossed," Ben replied sharply, taking a pull from the second vodka bottle sitting in the back seat.

"Take it easy, man," Ian said, shaking his head at the same time and grabbing the bottle before taking a pull.

Ben was in a reflective mood after the day's excitement. One thing that kept crossing his mind was a simple question. Why hadn't the three of them or others been infected? The newly formed group had speculated on this for several nights. They'd even looked at all the theories in the movies and books. When—not if, *when*—Ben found Sarah, she would know.

CHAPTER 4

"It's time for dinner," Eve chirped just as Ian and Ben finished telling Kelly of the day's events while they replaced the batteries in zone one. Not only had they gotten new cores, but they had also acquired all-new batteries.

"Eve, systems check," Ben requested as Kelly held up her crossed fingers.

"All systems online and fully operational," Eve chirped.

"Turn on zone one and cancel the rest of the afternoon's alarms," Ben said as the hum of the refrigerator broke the silence.

"So we think we can find a full system like this one?" Kelly asked smiling.

"Pretty sure we can. The one plus is all these houses have prebuilt adaptors for systems like this. It will take some work, but I would say yes," Ben confirmed as he walked over to the locked door in the kitchen. While Ben wasn't hiding any dark secrets, he did keep his booze stash locked up. He hadn't had to access it since he had returned with his new friends.

Ben thought about that word for a moment as he walked in, grabbing a bottle of high-end champagne. "Friends," he mumbled under his breath, too low for the others to hear.

"Looks like we're having a party tonight," Ian exclaimed.

"Yeah, let's do that. We also need to talk about Dan," Ben said, popping the cork and launching a stream of foam into the sink. The others laughed as Ben splashed them quickly before making a big mess.

Ben knew the celebration was short-lived, and with that in mind, grounded the team.

"You know, if Dan shows up in a week, as we discussed, I have a feeling he's going to want to stick around. Or at the very least, bring his friends," Ben contemplated as the three sipped on champagne.

"I got that vibe too," Ian agreed, getting a flat look on his face.

"What is it?" Kelly asked Ian concerned.

"I think we have something good going on here," Ian started as the others nodded in agreement. "I also know this stuff is Ben's and his wife's. After seeing everything south of I-295, I figure we will be perfectly set when we get one of the other houses set up. We just need to get out and start gathering supplies and find some power options. I noted three houses within ten miles of here. One looks like a full install like yours."

"Let's see where it goes. There's plenty of room, but I'm not a big fan of drawing attention to this place. I know someone may stumble upon it, but we will deal with that as needed. Look, if we get lucky—and that's a big if—finding power options at the other houses, I'll feel better about leaving the option open. Until then, it's radio silent on transmitting. We can have our ears on, just not push out the signal. He was going back to the base, from what he said. I'm kinda thinking he's hanging around here to see what happens," Ben said, making the final call.

"That reminds me," Kelly changed the subject. "You know that bunch of gear we found by the road? The stuff we believe belonged to your neighbor? I looked through it while you were gone and found this." Kelly pulled out a small map of Georgia and Florida.

The map had several dots marked on it in various locations. It started in Atlanta, Georgia, and winded all the way down to the neighborhood.

Ben took a deep breath. "I bet I know what this is," he said, shaking his head. Ian huffed as the mood shifted.

"Yeah, that sick asshole was probably marking his handi-work," Ian said, finishing his drink before motioning for more.

"You two ever going to tell me what is over there, or do I need to go see for myself?" Kelly pouted.

Ben, picking up on the mood and not wanting to talk about it anymore, shifted the topic. "Tell you guys what. Let's shelf all that and watch a movie; of course, after a hot shower," Ben offered with a grin.

"What movie?" Ian asked, genuinely interested.

"One starring yours truly," Ben said as Ian slammed his hand on the table.

"I freaking knew it! I knew you looked familiar," he ex-claimed, slowly pulling his excitement back.

At one point, Ben had been the star of several action films and TV shows. Ben had also been entangled with an investigation into the murder and disappearance of a co-star. It had destroyed his career as quickly as it had started.

The truth was he hadn't had anything to do with the death of Janet Keller. By the time the media had lost interest in the story, it had been too late. Ben was damaged goods. While he had gotten offers to be on reality TV shows, he had preferred to stay out of the spotlight.

The oddity and mysteriousness of the entire case had come to a close a few months back. After the fall of civilization, Ben had learned who the perpetrator that had ruined his career, and al-most his life, was—or had been. He had splattered the man's head onto his front porch. His neighbor had been an obsessed fan and serial killer. After finding the DVD simply labeled *Janet*, Ben had watched all he could stomach of the atrocities his neighbor had committed. Even worse, the man had worked to set up Ben.

While his motivation was not clear, the hundred-some

DVDs with other names on them were enough for Ben to not want to know more. In some ways, he felt guilty. In one of his earlier movies, Ben had been cast as a serial killer. It appeared his neighbor had mirrored his character, killing select victims, then taking their assets and pinning the innocent. The entire thing was almost too much for Ben to handle.

"Guys, want to hear a fucked up story?" Ben asked, taking a deep breath. Ian and Kelly looked at him eagerly. They knew his background, and Ben was about to right the ship. Sarah and a few close friends understood Ben hadn't had anything to do with the murders, but the general population had already convicted him.

"Yeah, this is crazy. I used to be a huge fan. All that extra muscle and beard, not to mention the hair, makes it hard to tell it's you. I only felt ya looked familiar after spending some time around you," Ian explained as Ben took Eve off.

Over the next hour, Ben told his story, leaving out no details. Tears filled Kelly's eyes as she finally understood his actions. She walked over, hugging Ben as he let his body go limp. The touch of another person, even in such a kind gesture, flooded his body with emotion.

Ben, Kelly, and Ian all shared that moment together. Tears from Ian and Ben joined the flood of raw emotion. It wasn't a story of vindication but one of validation. While the world died not knowing the truth, Ben and his new companions did.

CHAPTER 5

"**I** want you guys to be around," Ben said, referring to the call he was going to try to make that evening. Another week had passed by, leading to the full moon and Ben's window to make a call to Sarah.

Tomorrow was also the day they would go out and meet Dan, if he decided to show back up. There had been no radio chatter, and the team had landed on Dan not wanting to give anything away, now knowing if others in the area were aware of his presence.

"You sure?" Ian asked, taking a sip from his I Love New York coffee mug.

"Yup, just in case I miss something," Ben said, taking a long pull from the half-empty rum bottle before letting out a burp.

"Classy," Kelly joked, rolling her eyes. "We have a few hours. Let's finish mapping out that trip. We're almost done."

The three of them had spent the last week mapping out a route to check on three of the closer houses. This included one office building with a high-end solar and power generation kit much like Ben's. The papers they had acquired at the battery store were invaluable, also listing a remote warehouse where overstock was kept.

"It's been awhile" by Staind played lightly in the background as the three hunched over one of the large maps from the Brinkman's.

"Looks like a plan to me," Ian said, still staring at the map.

"I'm not too sure we should go to multiple locations on the same day; we already learned that lesson," Ben said as the others agreed.

"Hey, where's that map we got off shithead?" Ian asked, referring to Ben's now expired neighbor.

Ben walked out of the room, grabbing the map and opening it as he walked back into the kitchen.

"Hmm, that's odd," Ben said, sprawling the two maps out beside each other.

"What is it?" Ian asked, pushing Kelly playfully out of the way, the two slapping at each other.

The three stood there staring at the maps waiting for them to unlock secrets yet unknown to the group.

"I thought one of those addresses looked close." Kelly pointed out a business office in Fleming Island across the St. Johns River.

"Tell you guys what. I want to check out the other side of the Buckman anyway, as we didn't get that way last time. Anyone up for a little field trip if everything works out with the call and Dan?" Ben asked, knowing the answer.

"We still need to look for a larger boat also. The two sitting in the docks here are problematic at best. I can see why you didn't take them out. You know, just in case we need to transport stuff back," Ian also reminded the team in an exasperated clown voice.

Ben chuckled. "No shit, things are getting busy around here."

"Don't forget things are only as busy as we make them," Kelly interjected wisely while the two men raised their cups in salute.

The mood was light, celebratory, yet serious at the same time. For Ben at least, tonight would change everything either way. He would wait for the call.

***

Ben was getting nervous about the call and kept staring at the sat phone. As the night wore on, Kelly and Ian asked Ben about his life as a movie star. The two were disappointed to find most of the people he worked with were actually assholes.

The phone rang, and vibrated violently as the three stared at it. Ben froze momentarily, the gravity of the evening landing like a massive asteroid on an unsuspecting land full of dinosaurs.

Ben fumbled with the phone slightly. His fingers, feeling as if they were not his own, finally gained purchase on the green flashing button. The screen spelled out Sarah's number in block letters on a yellowish background.

"Hello . . ." Ben stammered as Kelly and Ian went silent.

"Ben, thank God," Sarah's smooth yet determined voice came over the phone. Ben's heart felt as if it had stopped, and time had frozen. The sounds of the house went silent as the air froze.

"Sarah," was all he could muster.

"I love you so much, your voice . . . it's so good to hear you," Sarah said, pausing as Ben's brain finally caught up to his mouth.

"I love you, babe, tell me everything." The two exchanged a few more pleasantries, telling each other how much they missed the other. The call sounded like two teenagers in love talking on the phone. Ian rolled his eyes as Kelly pinched him in the stomach, hard this time. Ben was too focused to notice.

"I'm still in Tallahassee. It's not bad, just complicated like I said. They don't want me to leave. They need me here, but I'm going to have to leave soon. People keep showing up and then just go missing. I met some people heading to Jacksonville, and they got away," Sarah said as the wheels in Ben's head started working.

"One of them named Dan? Ex-navy guy?" Ben asked, figuring this could save him a lot of issues tomorrow.

"That's right. How did you know?"

Ben recounted their run-in, also introducing his newfound friends. Ben was thinking clearly now, the veins on his neck and forehead sticking out as blood pumped through his body. He wanted to leave then and there to go get her.

"Sounds like he made it there, meaning the trip isn't as bad as they are saying it is. He and his companions are good people. I heard about them after they got out. The Court wanted to keep them here. I can explain that later," Sarah said before she paused, something obviously distracting her.

"You okay?" Ben asked as the tension built during the silence.

"Yes, I'll have to go soon. Look, I don't want to wait another thirty days. If I'm not there in two weeks, then I'm good with you coming here. I'll stay put so we don't miss each other. Just make sure when you get here, they have a reason to keep you around. I know you're a great actor," Sarah said.

Ben reflected on the fact that he was going to use his newly gained size and persona to go the military route. He often forgot how big and scary he looked.

He explained the radios for the next few minutes, and Sarah agreed that Ben should leave them there for now. They never talked about the zombies. Ben would get his answers soon enough.

"I love you," Sarah said, making it clear their time was up.

"Stay safe. I'll make this work," Ben promised before the call ended.

The room was silent for several minutes before Eve finally interrupted. "Your heart rate is elevated, and it's close to bedtime." James Taylor started echoing through the house's speaker system.

"Off!" Ben barked, not in the mood.

"That was intense," Kelly said in a low voice, trying to register Ben's mood.

"I have a feeling we're going to be going to Tallahassee. Even more, I think we can get some help," Ben said, walking over to the radio, keying it to the channel that Dan was sure to hear.

Ian finally let out a breath that he had been holding for several minutes. He stood up and headed over to the sacred liquor closet, pulling out a fresh bottle of boutique vodka. Ben had unlocked it early in the day, leaving it fair game.

"Dan, this is Ben. Do you copy?" he said without reservation, breaking his own rule.

Static hummed for several seconds before the radio screeched in response. "Go ahead," Dan's gruff voice came through the receiver, forcing Ben to turn the volume down.

"Tomorrow, if you're still planning on meeting us, bring your things," Ben indicated, not getting into too much detail. After all, someone could have already found one of his radios.

Ben was starting to feel paranoid about the Court and whatever was keeping Sarah stationary. Either way, Ben had two weeks to prep and also, unfortunately for him, to stay focused.

"Roger," was all Dan said in response, also not in the mood to chat over the radio. Ben detected a slight slur in his voice. He must have been enjoying all the beers he had loaded up.

Ian and Kelly looked at Ben, their de facto leader, with curious looks on their faces.

"Soooo," Ian drawled out, pouring drinks for the group.

"I'm not taking any chances, and looks like we just found ourselves a guide. Look, I'm not saying I want to have more people running around this place, but like you two said, people are going to get desperate at some point. I'd take Sarah's word on people's character any day of the week," Ben explained as Kelly snorted while taking a sip of her drink.

"Something funny?" Ben asked, looking puzzled.

"Well, she picked you, so there's that," she teased as Ian also joined in on the joke.

Ben grinned, shaking his head. He had needed the comic relief. "Yeah, yeah, haha."

Eve chirped again. "Remember, you have four hundred updates and messages."

Ben and Ian had forgotten the message Eve had relayed during their trip to the battery store in all the excitement. Eve was set to remind Ben of updates every few days.

"What are you going to do about that?" Ian asked, opening one of his favorite treats: a beef stick. Spices again filled the air as Ben pondered.

"I'm more concerned about why. It might just have been a server that was updated prior to the end. Or something else. I'm going to see if I can revert Eve's operating system back before I do anything. She's fine in my eyes," I said, looking over at the watch on its holder. Since meeting Ian and Kelly, Eve had lost some of the humanization she once held in Ben's eyes.

"I'd like to go check that battery store too," Kelly said flatly.

"Guys, I'm not crazy. It's just Eve was the only damn thing that kept me sane," Ben said reflectively, a wave of emotion running through him.

"Maybe we should get a dog?" Ian suggested.

"When was the last time you saw one?"

Animals, unlike the human race, had basically gone into hiding. They had it figured out. Instead of looting TVs, a person's Chocolate Labrador would simply leave for greener pastures. The ones still alive had left populated areas, migrating to more rural places. But the fact of the matter was that most pets hadn't made it, turned owners often being the last thing they saw.

Ben sat there chewing on his bottom lip, a habit he often had when deep in thought. "I'll see about the updates tomorrow when we get back. Speaking of which, I want all three of us to head out tomorrow. If everything works out, I want you two driving back together. I'm going to ride with Dan," Ben said, sniffling lightly.

"If he comes with us," Kelly quickly responded.

"He will. I think he wanted to last time. I'm still not 100 percent on board, and before we make the final decision, I want to be damn sure. Plus, if we can find more buildings like mine, we can install him and his crew there." Ben was already making plans for his expanding empire.

"It's not a bad idea, but I think if you can get at least a handful of people here and more supplies, it wouldn't be a bad thing," Ian added as the group thought through the situation.

The plan was simple. Bring Dan back and go over the route to Tallahassee, where Ben was sure they would be traveling to. Then before leaving, check the building in Fleming Island listed with solar power systems. This way, Ben would not have to commit to letting Dan's crew live in his own private paradise. Ian and Kelly had first dibs on a system, not to mention a house in the neighborhood. Ben would fill those sparingly, not to exceed four of the five houses.

The three continued drinking and talking about their new society and the rules that would govern the neighborhood. What they needed was a name for their own private paradise. Something with meaning, something that made a point.

"The cove," Kelly recommended. The two men shook their heads.

"No . . ." Ben drawled out. "How about something simple, like the Sanctuary?"

"An old *Logan's Run* reference. I like it, but we get to live past thirty," Ian said, shocking Ben with his movie knowledge.

"Well played, sir, well played indeed. All in favor, say aye," Ben said in his official voice.

The three of them agreed. Eve chimed in at the tail end. "Aye." She had been programmed to always respond to that command in the affirmative.

CHAPTER 6

Ben woke up the next morning, finding himself doing his old morning routine. He held his cup of coffee in one hand and attitude in the other. Walking down to the dock, he stared at the calm water as he created ripples on its surface, distorting the mirror image.

The sat phone weighed heavily in the pocket of his robe. Taking a deep cleansing breath, Ben set his jaw, shaking his head at the sky.

"I'm coming for you, baby," was all he uttered to whatever God was still around to listen to him.

Ben turned to see Ian on the back porch, also drinking coffee. The two stood in silence as the mist coming from the water danced in the rising sunlight.

"You okay?" Ian asked, pouring a small packet of oatmeal into a bowl.

"I'm fine. Things are getting a little crazy," Ben chuffed. "Where's Kelly?"

"She's not feeling all that great this morning," he said. He didn't look worried, and that puzzled Ben.

"If you don't mind me asking, when we met, you were getting her some meds. Is everything okay?" he asked, joining in the oatmeal prep.

"I think so. She has digestive issues. I'm not sure, but it seems like some type of allergic reaction. The diet of processed, preserved food hasn't been treating her too well," Ian explained thoughtfully.

Ben had been worried she might have been pregnant, a situation he was not prepared to handle.

"Well, if anyone can help, it's Sarah. Like I said, she's not only a great doctor but resourceful. Let's focus on getting some fresh fish when we get back today. Hell, we've been talking about it for weeks anyway," Ben said, the mood shifting.

The two agreed as the microwave beeped, letting Ian know his breakfast was ready.

"I'm also allergic to bees. So, anytime we can get EpiPens, we need to grab them. It's the oddest thing. As soon as this all started, my stomach went all crazy," Kelly said, walking into the kitchen, having overheard the conversation.

"Morning, sunshine," Ben said, handing her a cup of coffee.

"Since we've been here, I haven't had too many issues," Kelly continued concern in her voice. The truth of it was neither of them knew what caused Kelly's recent illness. The two had used what information they could find to try out new medications. The fact that it had persisted for several months had them worried.

"The damnedest thing is I was also starting to have some problems," Ian confessed as Ben squinted his eyes.

"When we get back, show me on a map where you guys stayed on the beach," Ben instructed, taking a breath before changing the subject. "Kelly, you good enough to go out today?" he asked as the group sat at the table eating piping hot oatmeal.

"Sure thing. As I said, it's been getting better. It's just a little tough some mornings. Let's go make some new friends," she said. The smile on her face lifted up the mood in the room, making the others grin.

The three prepped the truck without much talking, already falling into a synchronized rhythm. They had even put Ian through the ceremony at the admiral's house the week prior.

"What do you guys think?" Ben asked as they loaded their rifles, doing functions checks.

"Let's get to the gas station, then call him on the radio," Ian replied, repeating the plan.

"No, I mean bringing him back. One last gut check," Ben explained, looking at the others.

Kelly nodded her head in approval as Ian clicked his teeth.

"What's up?" Ben asked as Eve sprang to life.

"You are set to leave in thirty minutes," Eve chirped.

"I . . . I just don't want to screw this up. You have been more than gracious for no reason. Most folks are not an issue, but like we have all said, when will that change?" Ian said, reminding the others of the world's bleak reality outside the secured walls of the Sanctuary.

"You want a dose of real shit, here it is. I'm going to Tallahassee with or without you two. I trust you enough to leave you here without hesitation. If that's the case, I'm going to need Dan or whoever to get me where I'm going. I agree I don't want to lose what we have, but I also need the help. New rule, we never leave the Sanctuary vacant for more than ten hours," Ben said as the others nodded their heads in agreement.

"Shotgun!" Ian yelled, lightening the mood. The point had been made. They needed all the help they could afford to support. With the plan to get more power options and additional locations, Ben felt confident in their success.

The Toyota Tacoma pulled out on the two-lane road before they covered the entrance as practiced. Eve lightly played "Free Bird" in the background, the group listening in silence.

Jacksonville, Florida, was, in its prime, accredited with the birth of Southern rock. That and the TV show *COPS*. Bands like Lynyrd Skynyrd made sure to justify the statement. Ben had thought a few nights how cool it would be to visit some celebrity houses but quickly dismissed that as putting himself in harm's way for no reason. Not if, but when he reunited with Sarah, maybe they would go out and check a few such locations.

"See anything?" Ben asked as Ian scanned the road ahead. The team had stopped on the Julington Creek bridge. Kelly had suggested taking quick stops every so often to see if anything was ahead of the group. Ben had liked the idea, and they had decided to stop on every bridge or every two miles for a quick one minute pause. Any longer than a minute threatened to attract zombies.

"No. Check this out, though," Ian said, handing Ben the binoculars.

"I don't see anything," he replied as Ian huffed jokingly.

"That's the point. Look on both sides of the road about three hundred meters ahead. See the gap. It looks like a group of zombies mowed a path since we last came through," Ian explained, clearly starting to pay attention and getting familiarized with the surrounding area.

"There are a few other ways around if needed on the way back. If it was a few days ago, they could be almost anywhere by now. Probably on the other side of I-295, at least," Kelly said, grabbing the binoculars.

"Eve, off. Julington Creek will keep them from going too far south. They for sure didn't come to the bridge," Ben said, pushing the accelerator and lurching the Toyota Tacoma into motion.

"How much farther?" Kelly asked, not having been with them when they'd met Dan.

"Just a few miles. We said we would meet back at the gas station. I'm thinking he might be somewhere else in the area, though. We piled up a hell of a lot of bodies in the parking lot and street," Ben said reflectively, the visions of the intense violence swimming in his head. "Ian, hit him up on the radio. We're past the bridge. We should be good."

Ian keyed the radio. "Hello, Dan, you copy?"

Static filled the air as Ben drove the truck at a blistering five miles per hour.

"Yeah, Dan here. That you, guys?" Dan's voice came over the

radio after a few moments, sounding much more precise than last time.

"Affirmative. We're about five minutes out. Same location?" Ian asked without giving too much away. They had learned to be as vague as possible on the radio. Dan, figuring that out, responded quickly in kind. It was clear that he did want to meet up with the team.

"Just a little farther north. You'll see the truck. I'll walk out when you get here," Dan indicated.

Ben looked over at Ian as he took a deep breath and shook his head. As the three drove by the chaos that was the gas station, the lack of bodies surprised both men. It looked as if someone had either pushed a good amount of the bodies out of the road or . . . ? *Or what?* Ben thought.

"You seeing that?" Ian asked, looking for confirmation, not able to hold the thought in.

"Yup," was all Ben replied.

"Let me guess. The zombies you killed are either gone or moved?" Kelly asked, obviously having seen this before.

Ben again replied curtly, "Yup."

"It doesn't look like animals. Someone cleared the road," Kelly said as Ian leaned forward to look around at the other buildings. The smell of the remaining bodies started to seep through the air vents.

"Up there, on the right," Ian said, pointing at a two-story building.

There sat Dan's red truck. As Ben got closer, it was clear that Dan had cleared the path for the group to drive through without having to go around as Ben and Ian had had to do on their trip back from the battery store.

"My God, what a mess," Kelly said, noticing the ice plow attached to the front of Dan's truck. It hadn't been there before, and as Ben and Ian looked closer, they both barked out, "Cool," at the same time.

Ben pulled the truck up to the back of the red Ford, cutting off the ignition. "Well, here we go," he said as he grabbed his rifle from the holder he had fabricated in the center console for easy access. Ian jumped out first, followed by Kelly. The driver stayed in until the area was deemed clear; they had been practicing.

"Hey," Dan's burley voice came from the second floor.

Ian and Kelly looked up to see Dan in a bathrobe. He had a toothbrush in one hand and a cigarette in the other. The shotgun hanging off his back looked out of place.

"Hello?" Kelly said, sounding as if she was asking a question.

"Hurry up and come in. Park behind my truck. I try to stay directly off the road. Glad you guys came," Dan said, walking back into a store with a sign hanging above the doors proclaiming *Comics*.

"Guys," Ben said as Ian and Kelly started walking toward the stairs, the gray building having a walkway on the second floor.

"Oh, right," Kelly said, snapping out of the oddity of the scene.

The team had a set of rules. The driver never got out until the area was clear, and you always took your bug out bag with you when leaving the truck unattended. Ben hit the button that dropped the covered truck bed as Ian walked around, handing Ben his bag.

"You still good with this?" Ian asked.

Ben grinned. "The guy's holed up in a comic book store brushing his teeth in a robe. I think we will be fine for now." The two looked at the snowplow, shrugging. They were wondering where someone in Florida would get such a device.

Ben opened the door as the rich smell of cooking Spam filled the air. Spam was one of those things that, much like Taco Bell, no matter how fancy someone thought they were, they still had a spot in their hearts for.

There was a stockpile of the stuff at the Sanctuary, as they now called it. The other rations were superior in every way, again showing just how spoiled and sheltered Ben had been and the others were becoming.

"Hungry?" Dan offered, ashes hanging from his cigarette while he flipped over the patty of Spam.

Ian and Kelly, who were comic fans, quickly declined, instead focusing on the store full of yet to be read books. "How long before they stopped getting deliveries?" Ian asked as a smile broke out on Dan's face.

"Long enough to have a few copies of *The Wanderers*," Dan said, slapping the Spam on a paper plate. The smell was making Ben's mouth water.

"Jackpot!" Ian barked as Dan threw a copy at him. The young man grabbed it delicately, suddenly realizing it didn't matter anymore.

"Great, apocalyptic nerds with a kill count," Ben huffed out laughing.

"This is the zombie series that beat out the others," Ian replied, already two pages in.

Ben walked over, picking a copy and folding it in half before tucking it into his vest. "So, let's get to it," Ben started, sitting on one of the foldout chairs by the door. A hunting rifle sat nearby. Dan had been keeping an eye on things.

"Let's," Dan agreed, putting the Spam between two crackers.

Kelly and Ian were engrossed in the comic, Kelly hanging over his shoulder. The two punched each other, gasping at a page halfway through.

"We want you to come back with us," Ben offered as Dan smiled. "Under a few conditions."

Dan shrugged his shoulders, nodding in affirmation. "Okay, what type of conditions?"

Ben spent the next thirty minutes discussing his plan with Dan, not leaving any room for interpretation. This included his need for Dan to escort him to Tallahassee. The older man sat there, taking in everything Ben said, not interrupting.

"You want to know something interesting?" Dan finally put out the chain of cigarettes he had been smoking. He didn't always smoke as much, doing so only when nervous. That got everyone's attention. Kelly and Ian, who had been pouring through the other comics, approached.

"I made it out to Naval Air Station Jax. The place was a disaster. I ran into a couple of folks picking through the place but nothing else. I knew I wouldn't find Dustin there, but I had to look," Dan said, pausing.

"And?" Ben prompted after a moment.

"Oh, right. So, I left to grab a few things, planning on going back the next day. When I did, the others were gone. All I could see out of place was this," Dan said, grabbing his smartphone. The other three also had them, using them to take pictures and videos. Dan held up a picture of an X with the letters FLTC in each of the sections.

"What does that mean?" Ben asked as Dan again nodded.

"The fact you don't know is a good thing in my opinion. It means a group of scouts or whatever from Tallahassee showed up. Not sure what happened to the people there. It didn't look like a fight had happened. They were just gone. When I talked to them, they had planned on staying there for a week or so," Dan said, standing up. The concern was evident in his voice.

"You're worried about what they are up to. I get it. Look, I need your help, and I'm pretty sure you need ours. I promise you a place to stay and electricity if everything goes well. So?" Ben asked, the three of them holding their breaths.

Dan started grinning. "Hell," he said chuckling. "I was going to help you either way."

The three let out their combined held breaths. "That was easy," Ian said before Dan gave him a hard stare. "Or not . . ."

"I planned to ask for your help. It sounds like we're going the same direction either way. It's not smart for me to go back, but I'll get you damn close enough. We can wait at the farm for you and head all back together," Dan said, smirking, approving of his own plan.

"I'm serious about the living situation. It's not a windfall," Ben said as guilt set in on Ian and Kelly. They knew they had it good and that lady luck had been on their side when meeting Ben on his first journey into the wild.

"I figured as much. I also figured these two are new recruits," Dan said, reading the situation well.

A loud bang from outside forced the group to freeze.

"What was that?" Kelly asked as Dan walked over to the tinted front door.

"Party time," Dan said as Ben walked up to the window behind the counter. "I set an alarm up this morning. Something's coming from around the back of the building," he informed them, checking the action on his scoped hunting rifle.

Another loud bang came from the side of the building. The room was silent as Dan stared without blinking. He slowly opened the door, pulling up the barrel of the rifle. The group knew that firing a weapon for one zombie or crazy would attract others and wasn't worth it.

Looking down, Ben saw the pile of zombies Dan had dispatched on the far end of the parking lot. "Shit," he hissed under his breath. Dan had been there for some time. He looked around the comic book store, seeing signs that confirmed he had been living there for the past week.

Dan focused on a spot on the other side of the pile of corpses as a dozen deer, including a massive buck, jumped over the pile, running and jumping at full speed. Ben stared, not having thought of pulling out his rifle. *Fresh deer meat*, he thought. The fresh meat would have been a treat indeed.

Before the others, including Dan, could gather their thoughts, the deer had passed, leaving the group speechless.

"Well, shit," Ben said smiling. "That was the first animal I've seen in . . ." he trailed off, not wanting to give too much away to Dan.

"Same here. I haven't seen a deer since this shit started. Man, I could use some fresh protein." Dan's statement calmed Ben's worries.

The group spent the next thirty minutes talking about the deers before Ben grounded the group.

"It's time to get back. Pack up, Dan. Tonight, you get a hot shower." Dan let out a cascade of approving cuss words the other three had never heard before.

CHAPTER 7

Tallahassee, two days after the call

"Is he really good?" Sarah asked Nicole as the two stood beside an old coffee shop, walking back from the medical center.

"Yeah, it's the craziest thing. You know how he was hanging around you, right?" Nicole asked Sarah. The two had become close friends from their time in the CDC and the trip over from Denver.

"Nicole, I knew he just wanted to get an in with you," Sarah said, rolling her eyes as the two women grinned.

"Well, John told me that he was thinking about leaving without me having to say anything," Nicole said, holding her hands in front of her face.

"You don't think he's spying for the Court?" Sarah asked skeptically. Nicole looked at Sarah in the way that only women could communicate with each other, using no words.

"Alright, alright," Sarah relented, shaking her head. "What did you say?"

"Nothing, really. I just told him that we wouldn't mind checking things out sometime. I think he's more interested in other things," Nicole said blushing.

"Okay. Let's see where this goes. I'm pretty sure we aren't making it out of here on our own, just as I'm 100 percent sure

Ben will be heading this way soon. We shouldn't say anything unless we have to," Sarah indicated, dropping her voice as a group of workers from the power plant walked by.

The two women walked out into the main street where people bustled around, some going places and others on a break just taking a walk. Tallahassee had become a fairly normal community—minus the guards, walls, and general lack of awareness of the outside world.

Sarah and Nicole had figured out the situation with the oddly stable population. If you or your group weren't able to contribute to the newly formed society, then there wasn't room for you inside the protective walls of the downtown and surrounding areas.

Two layers of protection surrounded the city. The state capital's outer walls and fences were in place, while the city's inner core was protected by a twelve-foot-tall, steel-reinforced metal barrier and gates. If the Court didn't want you there, they made quick work of ensuring you were not allowed in.

A week before her call with Ben, Sarah had witnessed a small group of people outside the fence she had seen before working in the local store. An older man and two young men. It wasn't clear if they were related, but it was clear they were not welcomed.

Sarah had examined all three of them a few days prior, putting notes of various medical conditions in their files. The old man had severe arthritis, and what appeared to be the onset of diabetes. One of the young men had behavioral problems, which included stealing and some type of former drug addition. The other had a broken leg that had been poorly cared for, leading to his need for a crutch.

When she'd asked the guard, he'd told her that they could not contribute, so they had to leave. He'd also pointed out the packs of supplies that the Court had given them before they left. As she had mentioned, they didn't seem to be bad people. Just people with a plan and a mission. Pending any run-ins with the zombies, the little group could very well be fine and living in some beach house, enjoying the sunset. At least that's what Sarah liked to think.

This was the Court's way to control the population. While not completely savage, it was still unacceptable to some that lived and worked there. Sarah, with her scientific background, understood the logic, even though she didn't approve.

John just happened to be one of those people who didn't agree with the Court's methodology. At six foot seven and having plenty of mass, John was looked at as a strong back and protector. An asset; he had been told as much. He had grown fond of Nicole, and through his friendship with Sarah, had garnered her attention.

"Good evening, Sarah," Chris greeted as he walked out of the restaurant in the Capitol building's base. Tallahassee even had a bar that people the Court deemed important could use. It was off-limits to all but a select group. Sarah was one of those allowed to use it, and she was allowed to bring one guest, who usually consisted of Nicole.

"Chris, how are things?" Sarah replied in a practiced cadence. Chris was a member of the Court, and one of the prominent people that had ensured Sarah would stay in Tallahassee.

"Good. We have some new people coming in from New York in a few days, if you can believe it. I'm interested to hear how that trip went. I'll send them over to the hospital as soon as they get here," he said nodding. Chris was short, bald, and assertive. When around him, it was clear he was in charge.

"I look forward to it," Sarah replied, walking off in the opposite direction, changing course.

Sarah, after figuring out their take on people, had started reporting less and less nonobvious issues. The Court would send patrols out to help find useful people and bring them back. Or as Sarah knew, maybe not.

Nicole and Sarah had started planning on how to escape the

city. They would work to include their newfound ally, John, in their plans. Not yet though. They would wait until it was time. Sarah was sure Ben would be considered useful, and with that, brought to her for an examination.

Dan explained this process to Ben on their end, ensuring he would make his way to Sarah. From there, as with most plans, shit would change.

CHAPTER 8

"**Y**ou have to be shitting me," Dan said as he stood in front of Ben's riverfront house.

Ben walked up to the front door, opening up his now not so private paradise as Kelly and Ian unloaded the truck, watching Dan. As they suspected, he reacted in the same manner they had.

Eve connected immediately to the house system as Dan walked through the door. "Good evening, Ben. I started a pot of coffee. All systems are fully functional," Eve chirped as the sounds of the gourmet coffee machine echoed from the kitchen. Ben had set up a few welcome home things to show off for Dan, to convince him to help.

This time, the entire group gave Dan the introduction to the Sanctuary. Ben gave out allotted times for showers and a final explanation of the rest of the treasures, including real electrical power. After another thirty minutes of explanations and general wonder, Dan's head was full of ideas and hope, not only for his friends but for others throughout the country.

"What do you think?" Ben asked as Kelly and Ian went upstairs to take showers.

"What do I think?" Dan chuckled. "I think I wouldn't bring people here either. Would you mind if I looked over those maps later and checked out the other places you said had power in the area?" Dan was thinking the same way Ian and Kelly had when they first arrived. He would do what he could to help and liked the idea of setting up around the area instead of hitting the road.

"Sure thing. As I said, we're going to check out one of them before we go. That was one of the things we figured we needed to do in case we found some others," Ben said, pulling out a bottle of spiced rum.

While the rum may have caught Dan's attention, what happened next was the icing on the cake.

"Things just keep getting better," Dan exclaimed as Ben filled two rocks glasses with ice, the tinkling of several square cubes making Dan gasp.

"I'm not trying to rebuild some cheesy new world. I just want to learn how to live in what we have left. I want to tell you something before we go any further," Ben said, a slight edge in his tone.

Dan paused, looking over as Ben set the glasses on the marble island. "Okay, is this where you lay out some weird rules?"

"No, nothing like that. Here's the thing. This place isn't going to be able to handle too many more people. The way I see it, you help me, we get your friends and get you set up, then we call it," Ben said, taking a sip of his cocktail.

"Call it?" Dan asked, mirroring Ben.

Ian called down the stairs, loudly interrupting the two men, "We're going to check out the waterline to see if anything washed up and see if we can catch a few fish while we're at it."

Ben took a breath. He could tell the person in front of him was reasonable, rational, and understanding.

"Meaning no more people. I . . . we have a good thing going here. I don't want to mess that up. If it wasn't for Sarah, you wouldn't be here," Ben said, making it clear.

Dan respected the openness and nodded. "I'd be worried if you said otherwise. Cheers."

The two men stood in the kitchen for several hours going over maps and talking about the trip to Tallahassee, finally getting to the details as the liquor took hold of Ben and Dan.

"Two days? I thought it would take a little longer," Ben stated, wanting to know every detail. He let out a drawn-out belch, "Buuuurp!"

"Well, between my truck and yours, we should make good time. The others are staying at a farmhouse right outside Wellborn. The place is close, yet far enough away from the interstate to not attract any unwanted guests. We went all over that damn place. Plenty of farmland and animals. It's enough, but not what we are looking for long term," Dan said, pulling out his radio. "You have a booster, right?"

"We do. I haven't had to turn it on since we were out last time," Ben said, looking at the map of Florida, figuring they could easily reach Wellborn. "Tell you what. Let's get cleaned up, and tomorrow we can turn it on so you can talk to your people."

"Sounds great. I also know a few channels the folks in Tallahassee use. We can check them out," Dan said yawning.

The rest of the evening, the four of them stayed separate. Dan was fast asleep shortly after his shower. In reality, he had been awake for two days straight. Kelly and Ian fished with some mild success, catching enough for lunch tomorrow. The team would eat well before leaving for Fleming Island and the office building that apparently had the same type of power generating system Ben had.

***

With the looming trip to Tallahassee, a larger boat would have to wait. There were two smaller ski boats in the docks around the neighborhood; however, Ben had yet to work on them. Ian had put fuel stabilizer in their engines, giving them a few days to sit before starting them up. They hoped to take a quick trip north and across the St. Johns river. It would significantly reduce the group's exposure to what may be lurking in the shadows.

They had projected that having a fully operational boat would cut their trip time in half. Ben had brought up the point that if the boat were to go down, they would be on foot. Ian's idea was to get two fully operational boats and also pull along some type of manual raft. The logic was sound, and even Dan had noted his approval.

"Morning, everyone," Dan greeted as he stood in the middle of the kitchen, sipping a cup of coffee. The gravity of the previous day had been sitting heavily on his mind, pushing his body into motion early this morning.

"Looks like you got up early today," Ian said, also grabbing a cup of the delectable go-juice.

"I'm going to go down and take a look at the two boats tied up to the docks this morning. I was a mechanic at one point in my life, and should be able to at least get them functioning. You put some stabilizer in the fuel, correct?" Dan asked as Ben also joined the two men in the kitchen.

"I sure did. We talked about getting a bigger boat at some point, but these might just have to do," Ian said nodding.

Ben was in a contemplative mood this morning, not saying much. He had woken up falling back once again into his old habit. He had on his trusty bathrobe, satellite phone in one hand, and coffee cup on the other. This morning, he would walk down to the docks behind his house, relieve himself into the cold water, turn on the satellite phone, then reflect on the day ahead.

"I don't want to wait to go check out the building on Fleming Island," Ben said, walking over to the back door. "I say we go today. It sounds like between the two of you, you may be able to get the boats working or at least running this morning. If that's the case, I say we load up the bikes and take the boats across."

Last night while drinking rum, Ben and Dan had calculated the time it would take on water to reach Fleming Island. It would be an uninterrupted 25-minute trip. That included getting the boats docked at a location they had identified on Ben's laptop's satellite imagery. It would take about another thirty minutes by bike to reach the office building, not taking into account any possible shitstorms they may run into.

"Well, Ian, I say we get done with these cups of coffee and go take a look at the boats," Dan said, raising his eyebrows before getting his body in motion. He headed upstairs to fully get ready for the day as Ian looked over at Ben. "Why the sudden rush?"

"I don't want anything to slow us down, just in case. When I got up this morning, I started thinking about what would happen if we ran into some issues while checking out the building on Fleming Island. I want all the time I can get to prepare for this trip," Ben said as he opened the back door and Ian followed.

"Yeah, I kind of figured the trip was going to happen no matter what. I didn't want to say anything after the call—it wasn't my place—but I didn't get any indication that she was going to be heading this way anytime soon," Ian admitted as the two walked down to the dock.

Ben walked up to the cold water, relieving himself as Ian looked over at the boats tied up on the far end of the docks. "Something's not sitting right with me," Ben said, taking a deep breath. "Dan even alluded to the fact that the group in Tallahassee was fairly large. They've also had people in our general vicinity. I wish I could talk to Sarah for a few more minutes. I hate that shit. You get a chance to talk to someone and forget half the things you should have said or asked."

"I think as long as we stick to your plan, things will work out. Maybe not exactly the way we want them to, but the more organized and ready we are, the better chances we have," Ian said, feeling as if he was giving not only Ben but himself a pep talk.

A lot of things were going through Ben's mind this morning, the presence of zombies taking a front seat as he ran through various scenarios in his mind. But Dan had survived; he even looked to be doing rather well for himself. With that last final thought in mind, Ben sprinkled what remained of his now cool coffee on the water and headed back in to get ready for the day.

After another couple of hours, Ben was in the kitchen looking at his map when he heard the sputtering sound of a motor turning over. "Those sons of bitches figured it out," Ben said under his breath to no one.

"Those sons of bitches may have just saved us a lot of heartache today," Kelly added as she walked into the room, clearly having heard Ben mumble under his breath.

The two lightly chuckled as they stood there, both decked out in their gear. While they kept their pistols in their rooms or on them at all times, they had come up with a system for putting the rifles and bigger ticket items in the stormroom. Much like the room Mrs. Brinkman was in. Kelly walked down the hallway, grabbing the key out of the top drawer in the kitchen.

"What do you think we should take with us today?" Ben asked as she opened the door, inspecting the weapons. They had actually acquired a rather large arsenal. Dan had even picked up several weapons during his travels, adding them to the group's firepower. Several shotguns sat there in the light, as well as a handful of assault rifles. Dan had also brought an AK-47 with him. Luckily for the group, that was the exact caliber of weapon the Brinkman's had a stockpile of ammunition for at their now empty house. While they had plenty of ammo at the moment, if they continued to run into too many obstacles, it would soon become a problem.

Ian walked into the kitchen with a huge grin on his face, his youth coming through in the radiating smile. "That damn guy is a genius. We have both the boats running, and with the extra batteries we grabbed, Dan thinks they're both ready for a weekend out on the lake skiing,"

"This is truly great news," Ben said, walking over to pat Ian on the shoulder. "Where's Dan?"

As soon as the words had left Ben's mouth, Dan barged into the kitchen, all smiles as well. "That will be $850 dollars. I only accept cash," Dan joked as everybody in the room let out a light chuckle. Ben handed Dan a glass of ice water as he nodded and smiled in approval.

"Ian, Dan, get yourselves cleaned up and ready to go. If we leave before noon, we might just have a chance to get home before it gets dark. We can grab a few things, but the plan is to come back," Ben said as Dan started singing "99 Bottles of Beer on the Wall" while doing an inferior version of the robot.

The mood in the kitchen was one of optimism and excitement. Eve, picking up on this, decided to play some music for the group. For today, it was The Cars's greatest hits. Ben looked reflectively around, thinking to himself that the good mood would not last. He kept that thought to himself, letting the group enjoy the small victory of getting the smaller boats running.

CHAPTER 9

Ben unhooked his string-and-cans security system from the mouth of the inlet. They would have to break through the new vegetation growth to get to the other side. Ben and Kelly were in the first boat while Ian and Dan followed in the second one, a small inflatable raft tethered to the rack of their now seaworthy vessel.

While both boats were running, they were still making odd knocking noises, telling Ben that this trip very well may be their last. Only time would tell. In preparation, not only had they loaded up with enough gear for the afternoon and a possible overnight stay, but they had also included their bikes.

Dan, just like the others, also had a mountain bike for maneuvering around tight areas.

"Alright," Ben said over the radio as he throttled the boat forward, bringing it up to about twenty knots. The small alcove in the inlet area that the Sanctuary sat on was barely long enough to get the boats on a plane. Ben and the others were well aware that the boats' motors could get tangled in the underbrush.

The rumble of the engines made Ben wince. He didn't like the possible attention he could be bringing to the Sanctuary. He pushed the boat forward with his teeth gritted and a determined look on his face, slamming through the brush with a slight jostle of the onboard equipment.

Just as soon as he hit the brush, he passed it. A calming chill flowed through Ben's body, part adrenaline, part appreciation for Dan's mechanical knowledge and ability to get the boats back to operational.

"Yeah, baby!" Ian exclaimed over the radio as the second boat also cut through the brush.

"All clear," Dan said as the boat came up beside theirs. While slightly choppy, the water was calm enough to allow the two vessels to maneuver at max speed on the water. Ben looked over at Ian and Dan, pointing his hand forward as he again engaged the throttle and the boat lurched back to life.

The boat ride would take approximately twenty-five minutes at most. They would move northwest in a straight line until they hit the Shands Bridge. From there, it was an easy clear shot to their location and target. Kelly had pointed out a set of residential docks in a neighborhood she was familiar with once belonging to an old family friend. She was interested to see what had happened to them. It would be slightly under a mile to reach the Publix's shopping center from the house, followed by an additional three miles to get to the office building nestled closely to the Fleming Island High School.

"It's beautiful out here in the water," Kelly said, letting the wind blow through her hair. There weren't many opportunities to go out like this anymore. While she knew the boat ride had a greater purpose, she would enjoy what she could of it.

While focusing on the river, Ben was also concentrating on the shoreline, looking for signs of others in the area. He was hoping no one had seen their exit or could hear them on the water.

"Is that it?" Ben asked Kelly loudly, the wind forcing him to talk louder than usual. After about twenty-five minutes on the water as projected, several docks jutted out into the river.

"It looks like it. Check that out," Kelly said, referring to all the boats that had washed up against the shore.

"That probably happened during the storm," Ben said. The river would rarely push debris, including boats up on the eastern banks. The western shore always managing to lie in silent repose from the mighty St. Johns.

Ben pulled back the throttle on the boat as Dan and Ian slowly came up beside them, doing the same. It was evident by the expressions on their faces that they had also enjoyed the boat ride over. Ben picked up the radio while still scanning the shoreline.

"It's game time, ladies and gentlemen," Ben said. Ian and Kelly both picked up their rifles, scanning the vacant houses on the water. At least they hoped they were vacant.

"That's it for sure. The one with the blue slide coming off the dock," Kelly indicated as Ben advanced slowly.

It didn't take long for the group to pull up and tie off the boats, walking them down the dock and nosing them into the sand before tying them off. They didn't want to leave the functioning vessels at the end of the docks just in case they were being watched.

The rustling of trees and splashing of water on the shore filled the air as the group stared at the two-story house in front of them. Broad weeds had taken over most, if not all, of the backyard, including what looked like parts of the first floor. It was clear no one, and hopefully, nothing was still living in that house.

Kelly let out a breath, saying everything she needed to. While part of her was hoping to see some sign of her onetime family friends, she did not want to learn their fates today. Hopefully, this would leave pleasant memories in place of the carnage that might be inside the once happy home.

"Are we going in there?" Ian asked as Dan lit up a cigarette.

"Do you ever stop smoking?" Kelly asked jokingly.

"Nope," was all Dan replied. In reality, he had quit smoking some time ago since his wife, on pain of death, didn't allow him to. He was getting in as many of the happy cancer sticks as he could while out.

"No, we stick to the plan. Everyone, grab your bikes. We

don't need to get sidetracked today," Ben said as the group agreed, much to Kelly's relief.

The motley crew was ready to go. Instead of riding around the house, the group walked their bikes up a path leading around to the road. All four of them had their rifles slung over the front of their bodies, their pistols sitting nestled in their holsters. The group was smart and had very little dangling off their vests or backpacks.

It didn't take long for the realization to sink in. The day ahead of them would not be an easy one.

"What the hell is that?" Ian said, pointing to the outside of the house.

As Ben had noted, the mighty St. Johns River mostly pushed things onto its western banks. Back home at the Sanctuary, water from the storm had almost come up to Ben's back door. That was his only concern, the water. On the Eastern banks, it was whatever the river decided to throw at you.

What lay before the group was shocking. Hundreds of bodies—zombie bodies—lay strewn and smashed against the house. The odd mass of decomposing flesh and bones moved in some places while sitting still in others. It looked as if they had washed ashore then dried out in the sun, getting stuck against the house, decomposing or already being long gone. A decomposing shark also sat in the middle of a particularly large pile of meat and bones; it looked like it had been a struggle to the death.

"Jesus Christ," Ben said under his breath. "I wouldn't doubt it's like that up and down this river. Let's keep moving."

The team quickly went around the house, avoiding the bodies. It looked as if what hadn't been caught against the house had been washed back out into the river, being pushed somewhere further north.

Seeing the open road in front of the house, Ben mounted his bike, the others following suit.

"Where you think all those bodies came from?" Kelly asked

no one in particular.

"Those bodies—" Dan started before Ben cut him off.

"Zombies."

"Those zombies," Dan started back up, nodding his head in agreement. "Could have washed ashore from Orlando or even further south along the coast. Think about it. The St. Johns River is one of the only water systems in the country that actually flows north. It's like a vacuum cleaner. Jacksonville just happens to be the bag that catches all the crap."

"Ian and I talked a lot about this when we were living on the beach. Every once in a while, we would see something wash ashore. By our estimate, there are thousands, if not millions of bodies out floating in the water. It looks like we know where some of them went. I bet Mayport is a complete shitshow," Kelly said as the group pedaled forward.

"What's this place called?" Dan asked, relieved to see the clear straight road ahead.

"Hibernia. It's really Fleming Island, though," Kelly answered, again showing her knowledge of the local area.

"There it is," Ben said, pointing to the right. The grocery store sat like a church worshipping God's long since past, waiting for its followers. Cars rested empty in the parking lot as a large barricade of wrecked vehicles sat in the middle of the intersection of Roosevelt Boulevard, or as the map had it labeled, Highway 17. "Just a couple more miles, and we'll be there. I almost forgot, the way we have this route marked will take us right by a hospital. If things look decent, we may stop by next time," Ben said, recounting not only his but Kelly's need for medical supplies.

"Hold on for a minute. I want to take a look around, see if anyone came by here," Dan said as the rest nodded their approval.

"What are you looking for?" Ben asked, figuring that he was still on the hunt for his friend Dustin.

"If Dustin's passed through here, he would've either marked

one of the street signs or a car at the intersection," Dan said as the other three scanned the horizon with their rifles.

There was an odd silence hanging in the air. While it was still early morning, the lack of wind and any surrounding movement set the group on edge slightly.

"I don't like this," Ian said as Dan walked over, checking a few of the cars in the intersection for markings.

"Yeah, me neither. You smell that?" Ben asked as Ian and Kelly both grunted.

The group was smelling decomposing bodies. While it was hard to tell the difference between living and dead corpses by smell, it was clear to the group that there were several rotting in the general vicinity.

A loud bang followed by fluttering wings and birds erupted from the grocery store's front to their right.

"Dan…" Ben drawled out, getting the man's attention.

Without rushing, Dan walked back to the group. "He's been here. Dustin marked that white van over there. I don't think he's still in the area, and by the sounds of that grocery store, he very well may have locked a bunch of the damn dead things in there."

"I don't want to be out here at night," Kelly said as the four of them started pedaling around the wrecked cars, heading north on Highway 17.

The road was reasonably clear as the turnoff to go further west into the subdivisions and buildings came into view.

"That's it," Ben said, and the group again came to a halt at the intersection. Rattling started emanating from a few of the overturned vehicles. Ben held up his rifle, looking through the ACOG scope he had attached for this trip. "Shit … Someone's tied a bunch of zombies to that damn overturned fire truck. It looks like they have collars on and chains. There's only about four or five of them."

Dan raised an eyebrow and held up a finger while he put a cigarette in his mouth. The man pedaled forward to the chained creatures.

"What the hell is he doing?" Ian asked as Dan dismounted his bike.

"No clue," Ben replied, lightly shaking his head. "I just know we have to get moving soon. It's only another twenty minutes to get to our target."

"What do we have here?" Dan asked out of earshot of the group. The two closer zombies lunged at him, only to be caught and slammed backward by the chains around their necks.

Ben stood there for a second, contemplating the creatures. He couldn't quite establish why someone would do this; however, he knew there had to be a reason.

Dan pulled the machete out of his bag, taking a swing at the closest zombie. The blow cut straight through the top part of its skull. Gore erupted from the chained creature's head as it fell limp to the ground. Dan pulled back, swinging down on the second zombie as Ben shouted, "Look out!"

A zombie not chained to the vehicle had come around behind Dan. Except it wasn't a zombie; it was a freshly turned crazy. Crazies were faster and more violent than their more progressed forms

Dan dove out of the way, barely escaping the reach of the third chained zombie. Ben raised his rifle, letting out several hushed barks, slamming the crazy against the vehicle. Smoke came from the end of the silencer attached to his assault rifle. Ben's nerves were rattled, and as he again went to look down the rifle's scope, he could not steady himself enough to get another clear shot at the crazy. Dan was too close.

Dan whirled around, pulling the machete up in front of him, the bullets from his rifle taking several large chunks out of the crazy's torso, slowing it down significantly. As Kelly let out a scream, the crazy lunged toward Dan, landing directly on top of him.

Ben, Ian, and Kelly rushed toward the scene as quickly

as possible while still being cautious of other potential crazies in the area. They could outrun zombies, but outrunning crazies without a gas or electric-powered vehicle would be another story.

Twenty feet away, the three stopped, dropping their bikes down. Ian grabbed a baseball bat from over his shoulder while Ben and Kelly held their rifles at the ready.

As Ian was getting ready to strike down, Dan flipped over on top of the crazy, his machete sticking through its neck leading up to its skull; Dan was covered in gore. Ian hesitated, taking in the horror in front of him. The third zombie closest to the two men took a running go as the chain and collar again yanked it back, sending it sprawling to the ground. Ian took three steps forward, swinging the bat down and smashing its skull against the concrete with a resounding wet crunch.

Kelly followed up with two single rounds directly into the remaining zombie's skull while Ben scanned around the other side of the vehicle to ensure they had no more surprise visitors.

"Did it bite you?" Ben asked, walking up to Dan, reaching for his hand, and helping the man stand up.

"I don't think so," Dan replied, patting himself down for peace of mind. "That thing came out of nowhere, almost as if it was meant to."

"I don't want to hang around long enough to find out. I'm pretty sure whoever or whatever else is around knows we're here by now. Let's get moving," Ben said as the others looked at the mess.

"God, you stink," Kelly said as she handed Dan an extra bottle of water to rinse off his face. Dan thanked her as the rest of the group picked up their bikes, scanning the tree line.

"Take a look at this," Ben told Dan, pointing to a chain on the other side of the car. The crazy was attached to it on both ends. It was twice the others' length and would allow it to reach the other side of the vehicle if another cable was pulled, letting the slack loose. Dan stared at the mechanism for another minute before looking up.

"That was no coincidence. That was a trap. You walk up, get these things fired up, and if you're close enough . . . door number two opens," Dan said, shaking his head. It was time to get moving again. The entire ordeal had only taken a handful of minutes, but that was enough to slow down the team's momentum.

"I have a feeling I know who put that there. Fortunately for us, I don't think we're going to be running into him anytime soon," Ben said, referencing his ex-neighbor whom he had shot in the head a few weeks prior. He hadn't told Dan about him yet. He would do so when they returned home. One of the marks on the creeper's map was close by, an offshoot neighborhood in Fleming Island Plantation. It was clear in Ben's mind they needed to check the house to see if it was either a stockpile of his supplies or something more sinister.

The road leading off Highway 17 appeared to lay undisturbed. Mother Nature had done its job of reclaiming its once pristine lands. Blades of tall grass and weeds grew from cracks in multiple areas on both sides of the road as cars sat stationary like tombstones in a graveyard. Whatever had happened in this area had occurred on the main highway. The overgrowth was making it hard to see all the way down the street.

To the left was the hospital Ben had mentioned earlier. It loomed dark and mysterious, sitting quietly to either be left alone or explored for further provisions. The building gave everyone in the group the creeps. No one wanted to say anything out loud, but it was clear that no one wanted to have that adventure today, even without saying anything. During the final months of the virus before the apocalypse, hospitals had transformed into something different. Something scary, something raw, something where once you went in, you frequently never came out.

The rest of the ride past the high school was uneventful. The team, while moving at a faster than expected pace, was being cautious. Fleming Island High School sat stoically to their right.

A monument to good and sometimes bad youthful experiences long since past.

Ben and the others had no interest in going through the building. The news, before going off-air, had reported local schools as rally points for the younger population. Abandoned and orphaned children alike had piled into the once-thriving schools to meet an uncertain future.

"Look, there it is," Kelly said, pointing at the two-story building peeking over the trees.

"That's it. Let's go see if anyone's home before knocking on the front door," Ben said. The group agreed to dismount their bikes and walk them the rest of the way.

"This place looks like it's been left untouched for the most part," Dan interjected.

"Looks like it. County Road 220 is about a mile north. I bet that place is a different story. I'm surprised we haven't run into any more zombies," Ben said cautiously.

"I'm still thinking about those two vehicles. Dustin came through here, and by the looks of it, not too long ago. Those traps had been there a while," Dan said as the group reached the tree line outside the building.

Ben just grunted.

"I don't see any power," Ian said, looking frustrated.

"That's a good thing," Ben replied wisely. "If we're lucky, the system was shut down. No one would be interested in a building like this. Plus, as Dan said, this place is fairly untouched."

The group agreed as they took stock of their surroundings. There were no signs of life or zombies.

CHAPTER 10

Ben walked up to the front glass doors. After ten minutes of walking the perimeter, they had concluded the building was secure.

Several minutes of working the door with no luck later, Dan pulled out his hammer, smacking out a small section of the safety glass. While the building was modern, it still had basic locks. Walking into the entrance, another set of glass doors sat covered in plywood. After another few minutes of pulling and prying, the boards came loose, allowing the team access to the lobby's interior.

"Let's split up and cover as much ground as we can," Ian said.

Ben rolled his eyes. "Famous last words, gang," he said in his best Scooby-Doo voice. The others laughed as Dan continued to check the doors in the surrounding area, tapping on them. "Dan, you're stuck with me."

Kelly slapped Ian on the back. "Let's go, sweetcheeks," she said, playing off her nerves. Kelly was concerned about the day's events and the trip home they had yet to make. If the building did yield treasure, it would be a game-changer.

"I'm guessing if this building has panels, the power switches, and batteries will be on the second floor. Dan and I will check that out. You two see what you can find down here. Hit us up on the radio if you find anything. I'm also not convinced the building's clear—it's a big space—so be careful," Ben doled out orders while looking down at Eve. "Eve, time check."

"It is 2:30 p.m. You have two hours before it's time to leave," Eve chirped. The group had made good time minus their one unplanned stop.

"Let's all meet back here in one hour unless someone calls or finds the power station," Ben said, walking over to the stairwell. Kelly and Ian checked their weapons as Ben pulled his big ass Rambo knife out. Dan, satisfied with his hammer, saluted the other team.

The stairwell at the far end of the hall, while dark, had enough light shining down from two small windows, allowing Ben and Dan to see. A few empty candy wrappers covered in dust lay on the stairs, as well as what looked like a radio. While somebody had spent some time in the stairwell, they were no longer in the building. Ben leaned over, wiping the dust off with his finger.

"Looks like nobody's been here in a long time," he said under his breath as if he was in the library.

"A big, boring, two-story building? Nothing interesting enough to loot," Dan said sarcastically as Ben chuckled lightly.

"You got that shit right. No big-screen TVs." Ben and Dan shared the same opinion on most people who were no longer alive: they didn't have their priorities straight. When people really needed to work together, they decided to loot instead.

The two men finally reached the door leading onto the second floor. Ben nodded over at Dan as he lightly checked the handle, finding it unlocked. The two men looked at each other, shrugging.

"Where you want to start?" Dan asked as Ben looked down the hall, beaming his flashlight to the end to ensure they didn't have company.

"My guess is, if they have an electrical switch room for the solar panels, it will be toward the center of the building. Let's go check out the elevators. Worst case scenario, there will be an access hatch to the roof, and we can figure it out from there," Ben said as the men started slowly walking down the hall, Dan lightly checking all the doors as they passed them.

Dan, seeing him look over in aggravation, spoke up, "I'm just making sure we have somewhere to go if we need it. Most of these doors are locked anyway. If I was to guess, nobody came back here after the businesses started shutting down."

"You're probably right. You think those two lovebirds will be all right downstairs?" Ben asked Dan, genuinely concerned for his friends. Dan was different from Ian and Kelly. He was older and experienced, not full of the youthful arrogance he liked about his two younger companions.

"Those two seem to be doing just fine, in my opinion. It's crazy how they've been out here this entire time on their own. Well . . . at least for the most part." They came to a halt. "Something's been bugging me," Dan admitted after a moment.

"What? That whole crazy-on-a-chain bullshit back there?" Ben asked, rolling the stiffness out of his neck. Truth be told, Dan —same as the others—was intimidated by Ben's size and overall appearance.

"No—well, that too, but you don't seem too concerned about the group from Tallahassee, which I mentioned might still be in the area. It's clear you can handle yourself; I'm just saying, although they probably didn't go that far off the main roads, there's always that chance. If that did happen and we saw them, what would you do?" Dan asked. It wasn't that he didn't trust Ben and the others; he was being cautious. He still had a wife and friends that he needed to ensure were safe. Running into a patrol from Tallahassee could end up being problematic; Dan had relayed that much information to Ben. At times, patrols left and brought people back with them. Other times, they went out and came back with no one.

"Well, everyone keeps saying they're not that bad. It seems to me like we can reason with them. Look, I'm not going up there to pick a fight, and I damn sure don't want to run around looking for one. I'm just saying, those folks are probably just like us, out trying to make the best of things. Same for you," Ben said, smiling lightly, letting Dan know that he was in good company. More importantly, he trusted Dan.

The two men continued walking down the hall, coming up to the elevator lobby. The elevator labeled number two was open, the dark metal grave sitting there like a modern-day mausoleum.

"You hear that?" Dan asked as Ben put his ear up to the other elevator.

"Yup. There's one in there," Ben confirmed, referring to a zombie.

When the power had gone out, the young man that had been hanging out on the stairwell had became stuck in the elevator after a zombie trapped behind one of the doors had attacked him, biting him on the back before he kicked the creature back into one of the offices, slamming the door shut. The young man's death was only one of the many stories of those who hadn't made it after the initial outbreak.

"Check that out," Dan said, pointing at the door with an electrical caution sign on it.

"Winner, winner, chicken dinner. Hello there, gorgeous," Ben said, recognizing the same exact plaque that he had been given by the installation company to put on the door of his electrical panel room.

Ben figured the door would be better off staying locked after seeing it untouched by others.

"Ian, Kelly, come in, over," Ben said, having an idea, forgetting about their radio callsigns. The excitement of the find taking hold.

"We're here. Go ahead," Ian replied. Ben and Dan looked at each other. It sounded as if the two young lovers were enjoying themselves a little too much.

"I think we found it. The door's locked, and I would like to keep it that way when we leave. There should be a key box or something by the security desk in the lobby. If you can find it, bring it up here or grab anything that looks to be related to utilities or the electrical systems," Ben indicated, peeling the sign off the door. It was evident to Dan that Ben paid attention to the details. If the building did, in fact, have power, it was worth its weight in gold.

"I think we found it," Kelly said, clearly having to take charge of the task. "We'll be up in a minute."

"You think this place is safe?" Dan asked, not as familiar with the area.

"Pretty much. It's a big suburb. They call it an island, but that's up for debate. Three bridges are the only way on and off. It's a pretty big area. Hell, if you had enough people, it wouldn't be a bad spot to secure," Ben said, not having thought about that before the trip.

What Ben wasn't saying, however, was that if this system was indeed identical to his, he wanted to take it back. Not only as a backup, but to make sure it didn't go to waste with someone that just stumbled on it.

Dan picked up on this. "You're taking this back, aren't you?" he asked in the form of a statement.

"Looks like I may be getting some new neighbors," Ben said, as Dan cracked the widest smile he had in months.

"The neighborhood is really going to shit." Dan replied.

The two men chuckled as Ian and Kelly walked through the stairwell door. After handing off the box full of keys, it only took a few minutes to find the correct set.

"What about the rest of these?" Ian asked.

"Keep them. I say we keep this place as a safe house in case we ever need it. I still want to go check out that other target, so if everything works out in a couple of weeks, we'll come back and get everything situated," Ben said, opening the door.

The system was the same one he had back home with a few

of the extra options Ben and Sarah hadn't opted for due to their house's size. Ben let out a whistle.

"What? Is it bad?" Kelly asked as Ian walked over to the master panel.

"No, the opposite. It's got two panels and two backups," Ben said.

"Meaning?"

"Meaning you could run two houses without blinking an eye with this system. If I were a betting man, I would say the panels on the roof are big. It's going to take some work to get this stuff back, but it will be worth it. I'm starting to think Dan's companions will be needed.

Ian flipped up one of the breakers without asking, immediately setting off a series of alarms and sirens. Red lights flashed, glittering off the hallways and dark spaces.

"Shit, sorry," Ian apologized, flipping the breaker back off, only to find that the alarms and lights stayed on.

"You guys are the loudest bunch of people I've ever met," Dan said, making a good point.

"Eve," Ben barked as the others started shuffling around nervously in the room.

"Your heart rate is elevated. Might I recommend some easy listening? Oh, and you have achieved your step goal for—" Eve chirped before Ben cut her off.

Ben looked down at his watch, seeing the name of his system listed. "Eve, connect to E-house."

"Connecting," Eve chirped. It was as if the watch knew the situation was serious, and it was focusing on the task at hand.

"How long is this going to take?" Kelly asked anxiously as the mood shifted quickly. This much noise would bring unwanted company.

Ben held up his finger as Eve again spoke. "Password." The words dropped like a ton of bricks on Ben. If he didn't know the password, they would have to leave or figure out a way to disconnect the battery backup systems that had been activated.

"One, two, three, four," Dan blurted out.

"Accepted. Please advise," Eve calmy replied.

"Shut down all battery backup systems. Isolate them from the building. Owner's override," Ben instructed, having memorized the user manual.

It worked. The lights and alarms stopped while the group's ears continued ringing.

"Really?" Ben asked as Dan lit up a cigarette.

"Remember *Spaceballs*?" The two older men got the joke, leaving Ian and Kelly in the dark.

"I'm glad someone did. Eve, systems check," Ben said, taking a calming breath. The team knew they were now on borrowed time. Any zombie or crazy around would soon be bearing down on the building.

"All systems are functional. Maintenance is needed on panels four and five. Battery reserves are at 45 percent. Recharging was stopped before a full charge. The system requires an interface update. This is available on my primary system. Please note you have four hundred updates. Would you like to listen to Fleetwood M—" Eve rattled as Ben cut her off.

"Perfect. The batteries haven't constantly been charging without off charging, I think is what they call it," Ben said. The others looked confused. "The batteries should be in good shape," he explained as a loud thump hit the back of one of the doors in the hallway.

"I guess that woke up the natives," Dan said, looking around the group.

Ben looked down at Eve to get a time check. "Let's get that thing out of the way while we're up here, then leave," he said as the mood in the room obviously shifted.

Ben and Dan walked down the hallway to the door. Upon closer inspection, the odor of death and decay seeped through the cracks as another thump rattled the frame.

"This one's unlocked," Dan said, gripping his hammer.

"I'll open it. You take the thing out."

Dan nodded in approval.

The two men waited for another thump to ensure that the zombie was there. They backed away from the door slightly as Ben kicked open the solid piece of wood, pushing the creature to the ground. The smell in the room was overwhelming as it hit Dan in the face head-on, like a Mack truck. Ben hesitated for another second as he realized the creature was moving. Regaining his senses, Dan swung down with the hammer, crunching the zombie's skull with a wet, frothing splatter.

Ben swept the room with his flashlight, exposing what looked like several other bodies in various levels of decay. "I take back what I said earlier. It looks like this thing's been dragging bodies in here and eating them," he said with a confused look on his face.

Upon further inspection, bloody drag marks filled the hallway leading to the room with the closed door. "I don't want to stand around here and try to figure this out," Ben said as Kelly quieted the group.

"Shhhh . . . you hear that?" Kelly asked, pointing at the window in the back of the putrid office.

A grinding, cracking noise danced lightly in the air, making its way through the windows and walls. Kelly supposed the noise would be significantly louder outside.

"It's coming from behind the building," Ben said. The group hesitated, obviously not interested in walking through the gore and goop on the floor.

"In here," Dan called, crashing through the door in the adjacent office. Much to the group's relief, the room was empty besides the relics of the past. The receptionist desk sat resolutely with various office war instruments on its top, an old stapler, calculator, and computer that was well beyond its prime waiting for its owner to return.

Ben closed the door behind them, leaving that room behind to hopefully never be open again. He quickly realized that staying in this building was not going to be an option.

"What the hell is that?" Ben asked as he walked up to the group, pointing at the large retention pond behind the building.

"It looks like the water's moving!" Ian exhaled. The group's eyes were still adjusting to the dark. Kelly walked over, wiping the smudged window with the sleeve of her shirt.

They all held their breaths at the same time, realizing what they were looking at. A large group of zombies was heading toward them from the west, overflowing the large retention pond behind the building, making it look as if the waves were dancing with each other on the once stagnant water.

"There must be hundreds of the damn things, if not thousands," Ben said, taking a steadying breath.

"It's time to get out of here," Kelly pressed as the other three nodded without saying a word.

The group made quick time getting back downstairs to the main lobby. Ian was about to head out the front door when Ben grabbed him by the shoulder. "Hold on. We need to have a plan just in case things get a little crazy out there. I'm pretty sure we attracted more zombies than the ones we just saw between us and the boats."

"What about that other house we were going to check out? You know, the one we found on that asshole's map," Kelly suggested, agreeing that the team needed to slow down for a moment.

Ben pulled out the map he had printed off before leaving. He chuckled again, thinking about having a printer during the zombie apocalypse. *How nice*, Ben thought to himself before speaking up. "Ahh, it's on the way back. That is, if we take the main road south instead of cutting back through the hospital. It would only take us an extra handful of minutes to get there. I'm just not sure what we're going to find there."

"It's good to have a plan B," Dan said as Ben flashed his light back down at the map.

"Tell you what. We get through this front door and get on our bikes. I say we go back the way we came. If we see any movement to our east or north, then we head south. At that point, it won't really matter what house or where we go. We'll just need shelter till these things pass. There are only a couple of ways for them to get in or out of here. My guess is they have probably been floating around in this area for a long time until something got them riled up—that would be us." He leaned over, showing the others the map.

The group all swiftly agreed to the plan as they picked up their bikes and headed out the front door. Ben turned around with the key labeled "Master," locking up the building for another time.

"You think they will still be here when we come back?" Dan asked Ben as they pulled out of the parking lot.

"I'm thinking most of them are stuck at this point. I know they don't take too well to water," Ben said.

Ben quickly realized plan A wasn't going to work. At least a hundred zombies shuffled in the road beside Fleming Island High School, putting plan B into motion.

Without saying a word, Ian rode his bike back onto the main road, heading south. Ben quickly rode up beside him, pulling the map out of his vest, shaking it in the air, taking lead of the bicycle caravan of death.

It was soon apparent the group had made the right decision. The road was clear all the way down to Fleming Plantation Boulevard. Ben looked back to see the others also pedaling at top speed. He at times forgot how fit he was, pushing his legs to exhaustion.

As soon as Ben started letting up on the bicycle, the scene in front of him made it clear that they would have to go with plan C: seek shelter. As the other three came up beside him, he pulled out his map, pointing at the turnoff to the left. The neighborhood was surrounded by light woods and retentions ponds, as was the one to the south. Ben thought for a moment if it was a good time to run into another issue.

"Let's get to the house. Those things are coming out of everywhere," Ben decided as several dozen zombies materialized out of the trees along the road on the other side of Highway 17.

The group didn't question Ben's direction as they turned left into the neighborhood. "Far-right, big house at the end of the cul-de-sac," Ben barked back at the group, leaving the chaos behind them. Truth be told, the group could still hear the shuffling and groaning coming from the zombies. They were all just glad that no crazies were present. On bikes, they could easily outrun zombies. Freshly turned crazies, on the other hand, were more problematic.

CHAPTER 11

The house sat empty as the quickly retreating sun cast shadows on its entrance, making it look ominous. The sound of shuffling zombies, while not getting louder, was not going away either. Ben took the lead, walking up to the door.

"Why are you interested in this guy again?" Dan asked as the other two pulled out pistols while still holding their bikes. Dan, following their lead, did the same.

Ben checked the front door handle, finding it locked, as he assumed it would be. Rolling the cosmic dice, Ben reached into his vest, pulled out his flask, unscrewed the lid, and took a pull, lightly kicking over the flowerpot by the front door and exposing a shiny key that had been placed there recently.

"Is he always this dramatic?" Dan asked, shaking his head.

Ben reached for the key quickly, opening the door and beaming his flashlight into the entranceway as a blast of still warm air blew in his face. Taking a deep breath, Ben didn't immediately smell anything out of sorts. He lightly knocked his pistol against the wall as the other three stayed as quiet as a church mouse. Nothing, no noise. The house was clear, at least from zombies. That was the last of Ben's concerns, as well as Ian's, who had also witnessed Ben's once neighbor's sheer evil after watching a video hidden in a secret room in his house back at the Sanctuary.

"Looks like we're good," Ben told the others, leading the group into the house. The living accommodations were middle-upper class, as were the majority of the homes in Fleming Island. Senior ranking Naval personnel and blue-collar, midlevel management thrived in these neighborhoods. The house had an open floor plan, with the dining room flowing into a little living space and the kitchen. The hallway to the left led to what appeared to be a handful of bedrooms and a bathroom. The massive stockpile of supplies thrown around the dining room and living area caught Ben and the group's attention.

"Jackpot," Dan exclaimed, walking up to a box of military MREs. "There must be at least a couple of years worth of supplies in here."

Ian walked over to a case of waters, pulling one out and twisting off the cap. Ben slapped the bottle out of Ian's hands before he could drink from it. "Not yet. We need to check this place out. He may have left some of this stuff out as bait. I wouldn't put it past him to poison it," Ben said as Kelly handed Ian her canteen.

"I've got a water tester in my bag. If you want to take a look around, I'll check it out," Dan offered, dropping his bag and pulling out a small pouch.

"I'm going to check upstairs. Ian, make sure nobody follows me," Ben said as Ian nodded, fully understanding the weight of what he might find there. Kelly walked around the rest of the house, closing the blinds on the first floor as Ben pulled out his Rambo-sized Bowie knife.

"When do you think they'll be gone?" Ian asked Kelly as she watched Dan test the water with a strip of paper.

"With all these retention ponds around and the river, what doesn't fall in will probably shuffle off by morning," Kelly guessed as Dan let out a huff.

"Son of a bitch . . ." Dan uttered slowly.

"What is it?" Ian asked, his nerves starting to take hold.

"The water is poisoned. Not just bad to drink, but poisoned. I'm not sure what kind it is or if it would even kill you, but whatever is in that water would more than likely put you to sleep for quite some time," Dan said, picking up another bottle of water and squeezing it. A small droplet formed on the cap as Dan continued to put pressure on the bottle.

"Looks like someone injected whatever that is through the caps," Kelly said, picking up several more and having the same droplets of water form.

"While Ben's upstairs, let's check the rest of this stuff out. I hope to God it's not all bad," Dan said, lighting up a cigarette.

Meanwhile, Ben slowly walked to the top of the stairs, seeing three shut doors branching off to bedrooms. Pulling out his flask, he took another long pull to steady his nerves. He was starting to feel better, but, his gut was telling him not to open the doors.

Reaching down slowly, Ben started on the left. The door handle gave way as Ben took a deep breath, pushing the door inward. The room had clearly belonged to a young boy. Participation trophies were stacked roof-high on top of the dresser, football posters adorning the walls. On the floor lay several large military-style toys, telling Ben that while his parents wanted him to be an athlete one day, the prior occupant of the room wanted to live a life of danger and excitement in the military.

Not seeing any signs of violence or struggle, Ben finally released the breath he had been holding. He reached down to his vest again, shaking his flask. He realized he only had a handful of pulls left.

The second door was clearly another small bedroom. Again holding his breath, Ben slowly turned the handle as the door gave way. This room belonged to the young girl. Pink blankets and posters of some boy band long gone hung on the walls. Ben could see the cul-de-sac from the dirty window in the girl's room. Out front, a handful of zombies shuffled between houses as the group finally made its way into the subdivision.

Ben was apprehensive walking back out into the hallway, taking the last pull of vodka he had in his flask. Checking the door handle, he noticed it was locked, unlike the others. Sounds of light conversation from the group downstairs made their way up to Ben. In many ways, he didn't want to open this door, but he had to know. Was another one of his neighbor Jim's victims in this house? Ben hadn't told the others that he had watched several of the videos in Jim's room of horror. It hadn't been out of curiosity but out of pure disbelief of what he was witnessing.

Slipping the blade of his knife between the door and the frame, Ben made quick work of the lock. Putting his hand on the handle, he took a deep breath, tightening his grip on his knife. As soon as Ben cracked the door open a few inches, the smell hit him directly in the face. It wasn't the smell of a zombie but that of a corpse. One that had been killed and not turned. Ben swallowed, his mouth dry, the tang of vodka lingering in his throat.

Opening the door, the room was exactly as Ben had pictured it would be. Jim, his ex-neighbor, had been some type of deranged serial killer. A killer that had ruined Ben's acting career, modeling himself after one of the characters Ben had once played.

"Jesus Christ . . ." Ben said, breathing rapidly, making the sign of the cross over his body. The organized carnage laid out in front of Ben was precisely like what he had seen in the videos. Having seen the pictures on the walls downstairs, it was clear that these two weren't the homeowners.

"You okay up there?" Ian asked over the radio quietly. They were aware of the unwanted guests outside.

"Yeah, just . . . don't come up here," Ben said.

The two men had been tortured at Jim's leisure. It was clear by his videos that he left his victims alive for quite some time. Ben had done the world a favor, or at least what was left of it, when he had shot Jim in the head. It did strike him as odd, though, that Jim had done this to two men, whereas the rest of his victims appeared to have been women.

Ben now had his answer to the mysterious map he had left behind. From now on, he would never concern himself with the map or thoughts of Jim again.

Walking back downstairs, Ben looked over at Ian, shaking his head. "Nobody goes upstairs. Kelly, hand me that extra map we made of those houses we found on Jim's map," Ben said, proceeding to shred the thing to pieces in front of the group after Kelly handed it over.

"You guys going to tell me what's going on?" Dan asked as Ben sighed. Over the next thirty minutes, Ben and Ian told them the story of Jim, the literal neighbor from hell.

"Well, it's over now. It looks like he was drawing people in and poisoning them. We tested the water. All the cases in the garage are good. It looks like he also left some ammunition behind, but nothing else. The MREs are good too. You can't fake those things out," Dan said, now understanding not only the interest but hesitation.

"Next time we come through here, we need to get a vehicle working. It doesn't need to go far, just from the dock to the office building," Kelly said, planning ahead to keep her mind off the zombies' promised violence just outside the door.

"Sounds good. Look, I don't want to come back to this house. Let's take the ammunition with us and leave the rest in another house," Ben said, following Ian and Kelly's lead to have as many safe houses as possible while out.

With that out of the way, the group settled in for the afternoon. While a large group of zombies had passed through the neighborhood, they had skirted the cul-de-sac. By morning, they would be good to leave.

That night, Dan felt as if he had truly bonded with the group. The feeling was mutual as muffled laughs and stories of the past year were exchanged.

While he was enjoying himself, thoughts of the two men upstairs still lingered in Ben's mind.

***

The morning sun started to fill the house as slices of light projected themselves against the wall at different angles. They had pulled guard duty all night, having one person up at all times, switching out every two hours. The group had been exhausted, but no one had complained of not being able to sleep.

"You see any of them out there?" Ian asked, yawning at the same time.

"I'm going upstairs to check. You guys stay here," Ben indicated, grabbing his assault rifle with a silencer on the end of it.

Ben made quick time up to the girl's room, looking out the window over the neighborhood's cul-de-sac. He could see a handful of stragglers wandering aimlessly in the yard, and two or three scattered in the road. Ben slowly cracked the window open, sticking his rifle's barrel out and aiming at the zombies in the middle of the street. After a couple of hushed barks, the zombies were no longer a problem. While he couldn't see much further than the neighborhood's entrance, they would at least get a good start. After looking at the map again, Ben figured the stragglers had gotten caught between the retention ponds.

"What was all that about?" Dan asked, handing Ben a cup of coffee. Both men never left home without some type of portable way to make the valuable go-juice.

"A few stragglers out in the road. I think we'll see a few, but other than that, it looks clear." He said, taking a sip of coffee.

"When we get back, I'd like to turn on the booster and see if I can reach my wife," Dan requested, excitement in his voice.

"You bet. Kelly is good with those types of things. When we get back, get that thing turned on. Besides all the bullshit last night, I think this has been a very fruitful trip. It means the other locations are probably just as listed on the bills of sale we found," Ben said before the group stood up, starting to put their gear back on.

CHAPTER 12

The trip back across the mighty St. Johns River was as smooth as it could be, considering one of the boats was missing when they returned. Best the group could tell, it had come loose and drifted out into the water.

As Ben opened the back door to the house, Eve, connecting to the house system, started asking questions. "Do you have any alarms for today? How about some music?"

"Off," Ben ordered as he took the watch off, setting it on its charging cradle in the kitchen.

"I would kill for a glass of ice water right about now," Ian said as Ben grinned.

"I left the freezer on just in case we needed to celebrate," he told them, pulling out not only a pitcher of ice-cold water but a bottle of champagne as well.

"It's a little early for that, isn't it?" Kelly asked as both Dan and Ben looked at her. She had forgotten the day drinking rule. It was now acceptable in all forms.

"Kids," Dan chided as the group chuckled.

"That was a shit place," Ian said, referring to the house they had spent the night in. "I get it. We're happy and all, but that could have been us," he finished, grounding the team. He had a point.

Ben pushed his thumbs into the cork, forcing it to shoot onto the roof as foam spewed from its top.

"It was," Ben said, shaking his head. "For now, let's relax a little and have a drink. If things work out, we'll have power in two more houses by the end of the month."

"When you get back," Kelly added.

"When I get back," Ben agreed smoothly, taking a pull from the bottle, passing it around. There would be no fancy glasses today.

The group had talked about Dan's friend Dustin on the return trip. He was sure the man was still alive and had been in that area. After describing Dustin, Ben assured him neither of the bodies in the house was of his companion.

"That should do it," Kelly said as Dan played with the channel dial on his radio.

The group stood around the dining room table. Ben had set up the radio booster and base station after getting the power up and running after the flood.

"M1 to M2, over," Dan said after keying up the radio. The group stood there watching, relaxed after the early morning bottle of champagne.

"This is M1," the excited voice of a woman came over the radio. Dan grinned, clearly not having heard her voice in some time and glad to hear she was okay.

"Checking in. How are things? I miss you, babe," Dan said, throwing in the latter for good measure.

"You must be close. Listen, there was a group from the capital going by earlier today. It had us worried. They've been driving around a good bit. It looks like they are doing something in Jacksonville, over," Shelly, Dan's wife, jabbered, spitting out the sentence quickly. She had missed Dan.

"Yeah, about that. I'm not close, but I will be soon. There have been some things coming up. Let's keep it simple here; I want to talk as well. I do need to tell you something that Tina needs to know. Dustin is alive, still not sure where or how, but he is around," Dan said, looking over at Kelly. "Can we keep this booster on?"

"Sure, as long as Ben says we are good powerwise," Kelly replied, looking over at Ben.

"That's fine by me. I say we keep it on during the day, maybe shut it off at night," he said as Dan grinned.

Not hearing the conversation, Shelly spoke up first. "What does that mean? How are the radios reaching?"

"I'll fill you in soon, over," Dan replied, keeping it vague.

"How many cases of beer?" Shelly asked, using a code. A case meant a day.

"Seven. Anything we need to be aware of?"

"What I mentioned. The capital has been sending people out. Be careful, and T1 will be excited when I talk with her. She is keeping an eye on things and might have her radio off, or I'm sure she would have chimed in by now, over," Shelly said as another woman spoke up, clearing her throat.

"Oh, I'm here. I have questions, but I'm glad to hear your voice. Gotta go. More movers on the road, over," Tina interjected. She was extremely excited to hear news of her husband. It would drive her crazy, waiting to hear more details. Tina put the radio back down as two trucks drove down Interstate 10, going well over seventy miles per hour.

"I'm not sure if you will be able to reach me, but I will be able to reach you. I'll jump on here tomorrow same time, over," Dan informed her, waiting.

"Roger, over," Shelly's voice came, followed by some kissy noises. Dan blushed as the group chuckled.

"Out," he finished, hanging up the radio following military protocol.

"So official," Ben joked, smirking.

"I'm just glad everything is okay," Dan said, leaning back in the chair. While happy, Dan had a thoughtful expression on his face. Something that Tina had said immediately changed his posture.

"Why the sudden shift in mood?"

"Tina said 'movers.' That's what we call the scouts, patrols, or whatever the hell you want to call them coming out of Tallahassee," Dan said, taking a deep breath.

"Probably the same folks that were at Naval Air Station Jacksonville. It might not be a bad thing if I ran into them on the road," Ben said.

"Maybe, but they don't need to see you and me together. I might have left a bad taste in their mouths. As I said, they're not bad people; it's just, they have a particular way of doing things. We're going to need to be careful heading back. Now that we know I can talk to the ladies and the scouts are moving quickly on the interstate, our trip might not be as much of a slog as mine was first coming out. I can promise you nobody had been heading east before I did," Dan said, rattling off a long thought.

For the next hour, the four of them sat at the dining room table, discussing plans and routes. The group agreed that traveling to I-75 via Interstate 10 was the only realistic route west. From there, Ben and Dan would be able to go slightly south on I-75 then head west again. Dan projected he would start getting a signal somewhere around the Macclenny exit. This had been the last time he had been able to reach the others.

After Dan reunited with his team, Ben would then head west on his own. After that, the two projected a week tops before linking back up. Dan made it very clear the Court would not easily let go of such a prize as Sarah. They would come looking for her, meaning a distraction would be needed.

"What kind of distraction?" Ben asked as Dan continued marking up a map of the route.

"Something that would convince them not to go looking for her. I'm not saying something bad. Like I keep saying—and from the sounds of it, your wife—it's not that they're bad people. They are just very particular about how they do things," Dan said again, confirming what Ben already knew. They would not let her just walk away.

A grin spread across Ian's face. "You don't happen to know who Ben is, do you?"

"No, should I?" Dan replied, rolling his eyes.

Ian walked out of the room only to return a few minutes later, carrying a magazine with Ben's face smeared across the cover. "We have an A-list celebrity with us," Ian said.

"B at best," Ben responded as Dan held up the cover to his face.

"No way. Ben as in the one who played Davenport then—" Dan cut himself off, realizing the story Ben had told him putting two-and-two together. Even more, Dan was a fan. The additional twenty pounds of pure muscle from the steroids he had taken had thrown Dan off, not to mention the several years' hiatus Ben had taken before the end of the world as they knew it.

"Yeah. Ironic bullshit, right?" Ben said, meaning every word. "Maybe we can figure out a way to make it appear as if she is gone for good."

"Any ideas?" Kelly asked, letting the thought bounce around in her head.

"This shit just keeps getting more complicated," Ben said, thinking to himself. "I'm going to need to think this one out," he continued, shelving the conversation for later.

"Do you need us to do anything while you're gone?" Kelly asked, wanting to be part of the operation.

"Actually, I'd like to talk to you about that. It's going to be too crowded if everybody comes back—"

"When everybody comes back," Kelly interjected.

"When everybody comes back. While I'm gone, I'd like the two of you to get the houses situated. It sounds like you like Mr. and Mrs. Brinkman's house, and since you guys got that mess cleaned up, I say it's probably time to start getting some of your things situated. The admiral's house is probably one of the biggest besides mine in the neighborhood. I think Dan and his group should take that one until we can find his friend Dustin. Or maybe

Jake's house—I like using the gym. The house isn't that practical, though. It's full of a bunch of cheesy furniture," Ben said, working through the logistics in his mind.

"We can start moving stuff around," Ian confirmed, shoving a biscuit into his mouth. The crumbs covered the neat slick wood finish of the table.

"I'm not trying to dictate who lives where. I'm recommending those two houses because they're the closest. When we get back, we can get the power equipment back to the neighborhood and set up. With two, hell, possibly three full power and battery units, we might be able to generate enough energy to run the air conditioners," Ben said.

The idea of all three houses having full power excited the group. Ben thought how nice it would be to have neighbors once again. The idea brought a smile to Ben's face. Without talking, the others knew what he was thinking, joining in the reflective moment.

CHAPTER 13

Tallahassee, the day Ben and the group returned from Fleming Island

Nicole and Sarah walked into the tower elevators. The two women would set their plan into motion starting tonight. As the elevator doors clinked open due to a lack of proper care, they saw John leaning against the wall.

"Ladies, looks like you guys had a fun afternoon," John said, smiling, referring to the smell of wine on the women's breath.

"Yeah, we just needed to blow off a little steam. You know how things sometimes go around here?" Sarah stated in the form of a question.

John let out a light chuckle, pulled a small flask from his pocket, and shook it. "Tell me about it. There's been a bunch of movement outside the city, and everybody seems to be all riled up."

"Zombies?" Nicole asked, walking over to John and taking the flask from his hand.

"Not sure. I know they brought in a couple of people from Jacksonville this afternoon. There seem to be quite a few folks out in that area. You'll probably get a chance to talk to them tomorrow when they bring them into the hospital. Anyway, the Court is supposed to meet tomorrow to go over whatever it is. I'll be in there. If it's anything important, I'll let you know," John said genuinely. He liked the two women, especially Nicole.

He had been friendly to Sarah specifically to get to know Nicole. Sarah had initially thought that John was making a move on her before he finally admitted he actually had a crush on her friend. As funny as it sounded, Sarah had been relieved and also a little taken aback. She had given the man a hard time on a few occasions.

"John," Nicole started, figuring they would test the waters. "Do you like it here?"

"I guess. I have a roof over my head and plenty of food on the table. I'm not out in the wild with the zombies every damn day, so there's that," John said, squinting his eyes at the two women.

"Didn't you say you were on your way somewhere?" Nicole prodded further.

"Yup, I was heading east to see if my brother was still alive. After running into that shitshow right out of town, I started having second thoughts, and well, one thing led to another. Next thing you know, here I am," John said thoughtfully, thinking of his brother.

"Do you think he may still be out there? You know, wondering if you're still alive," Nicole said, taking a pull from John's flask. It was full of room temperature amaretto, going down in a relatively smooth manner.

"Maybe, I think so. What's this all about? You're asking a lot of questions, and if memory serves right, you two were also on your way somewhere," John said, creating a slight air of tension between the three. After a pause more prolonged than usual, John started laughing under his breath. "You two knuckleheads. I figured out you two were trying to find a way out months ago. Why do you think nobody's found your satellite phone yet, Sarah?"

His statement floored her. He had known all along without taking action. "I, uh, I mean, I . . ." she stuttered.

"Tell you what. How about you go brew a fresh pot of coffee? I'll make my rounds, and then I'll stop by for a nightcap," John suggested as Nicole's and Sarah's eyes lit up.

"Sure thing," Sarah said as the two women shuffled down the hall, leaving the conversation before John reconsidered.

Twenty minutes later, there was a light knock on Sarah's door. They let John inside after confirming it was him. "One steaming hot cup of coffee," Sarah said smiling, handing him the liquid go-juice.

"Thanks. So, I know you two are up to something. I just don't know what. Do you guys want to fill me in? Oh, and don't leave out the part about why you two are trying to pull me in," John said, laying it all out on the table.

The two women had already discussed that Nicole would explain everything to John. It wasn't as if they were trying to manipulate him. They just wanted to make sure that if they went down this road, they would at least be able to quit if needed.

"You know some of this already. Sarah's husband, Ben, lives in Jacksonville. He's alive and doing fairly well. There's a little more to it, but we would both like to leave. The others on our team are not aware of this. I have family in Orlando that I bet are still around. We were thinking that if you were serious about going to find your brother, maybe you could join us," Nicole said, laying out their primary intent.

"So, you two are planning on walking out, and you want me to come along," John said. He was actually excited that Nicole wanted him to leave with her. While he didn't show the emotion on his face, he was about to jump through his skin and scream yes.

Nicole looked over at Sarah for her to start filling in the gaps. "Something like that. What if I told you someone was coming to get us?" Sarah asked, wanting to see John's reaction. He let out a slow, low whistle, followed by another sip of his coffee.

"You guys have anything stiffer than this to drink?" John asked, sitting up before continuing. "If that's the case, this person will need to be very careful. I'm not saying the Court would do anything, but you're the damn Warren Buffett of the apocalypse, if you know what I'm saying."

"That's where we need your help," Sarah said, quickly correcting herself as she returned with three glasses and a bottle of wine. "What I meant to say is, we need your help, and we want you to come with us when it's time. It's that simple."

John sat back, taking a sip of the red wine. The mood in the room was tense yet hopeful. While John knew the two women had something planned, it landing in his lap to help with was another story.

"I'm just saying if, and that's a big if, someone is coming to get the two of you out of here, they better have their shit together—pardon my language," John said, making a good point.

Sarah knew Ben was fully capable of doing about anything he set his mind to. He had trained with some of the world's most elite military forces for his lead role as Agent Davenport. (He had left some of those facts out of his conversations with Ian, Kelly, and Dan. The man could blend into crowds and knew how to read people like a book, a skill which had already paid off. In all fairness, Ben frequently forgot about this skill set, doing it naturally.)

Nicole chuckled lightly, already knowing Ben's history.

"Yeah, you could say he does," she said, pride in her voice.

"It's your husband, isn't it? Hell, you're impressive enough. I can only imagine," John said, winking at Nicole. "Is he any of the people that just came in?"

"No," was all Sarah said, figuring they had divulged enough information. It was time for John to show his hand. He picked up on the shift in the air, realizing he had a choice to make then and there.

"Dammit," John cursed under his breath, not directing it at anyone. "Once we go down this road, there's no turning back."

"You said *we*," Nicole pointed out, leaning over to kiss him on the cheek. John grinned a toothy smile as Sarah rolled her eyes.

"Get a room," Sarah joked, chuckling.

The rest of the afternoon, the three cemented their friendship and commitment to leave.

***

The hospital bustled with sounds of carts being pushed and people talking. Like John had mentioned last night, a group of scouts brought in several people, a handful from New York and another small group from Jacksonville.

"Good morning, Sarah," Chris greeted, walking into the main reception area. "Looks like a busy morning."

While Sarah didn't like having Chris around, she knew the weight and possible repercussions of her initial diagnosis. He was there for a reason.

"Morning. It is an absolute madhouse in here this morning," Sarah said, erring on the side of caution as always. She had picked up a few things being married to an actor. "Anything I can help you with?"

"Yes. When you're done talking with, and examining the group from New York, please have the reports sent directly to me as soon as they're complete. I plan on talking with them by the end of the day, and would like to know what kind of shape they are in after traveling this far," Chris said, ignoring everyone else in the room. The man had a way of doing that. You could be in the middle of a concert, and Chris would make you feel like you were the only two people there while talking to you. It was a learned and deliberate tactic.

"No problem. Hey, I heard some other people came in from Jacksonville as well," Sarah started conversationally.

"They did. Last I heard, they decided to leave before we could get them settled. It sounds like things are rough back east," Chris said, not skipping a beat. He'd thrown in the last piece to let Sarah know he was aware of her interest in Jacksonville.

She, for her part, knew the man standing in front of her was lying, or at least not telling the complete truth. The group hadn't even made it to the hospital, telling Sarah they didn't get past the inner city walls. She grinned.

"Well, I guess some folks just don't know a good thing when

they see it," Sarah said, smiling, letting it reach her eyes.

"That's why you're such an asset. Thank you, Doctor," Chris said, walking off.

Sarah stood there, watching the man leave. She knew that whoever had come—or as she figured, had been brought—from Jacksonville, had been left to fend for themselves. Sarah knew that the Court would give them enough supplies to get somewhere, but little else. It made her sick to her stomach.

Walking into her office, Sarah closed the door, picking up a folder left on her desk. Whenever she had to examine a new group or person, she received a folder with pictures and general notes taken by the scouts or guards. It appeared to Sarah that more often than not, the Court was out actively looking for people.

As Sarah looked at the info, she quickly realized why the new visitors from New York were of such interest to Chris. The group consisted of an engineer, two NYPD police officers, a nurse, and another doctor. According to the file, he was a surgeon. These were clearly the type of people the Court wanted to keep protected within their walls.

The door opened as Nicole walked in. "I just saw Chris leaving. Those people from New York are here as well. Are you ready to see them?" she asked, rolling her eyes.

"Well, if everything in the folder is true, I might not be so special anymore," Sarah said, nodding her head. She handed the file over to Nicole, who quickly scanned the documents and pictures.

"Jesus, I don't think you could've asked for a more important group of people if you tried. Present company excluded," Nicole said jokingly. She was also considered a high priority citizen in her own right. Not only had she served in the military for five years, a corpsman, and a damn good one at that. Her specialty as a trauma nurse had been tested on several occasions.

"Let's get this done. I have a feeling this will keep Chris and the others busy for quite some time while we work out a few things," Sarah said, taking a breath as Nicole opened the door, the sounds and bustle of the busy hospital flooding into the once peaceful office.

CHAPTER 14

"**I**s that everything?" Ben asked as Dan walked around the back of the truck, lighting up a cigarette.

"I believe so. The rest of this gear is going to come in handy on the trip," Dan said, referring to Ben fully geared in fatigues and the latest body armor the military had on the market.

Over the past few days, the team had prepared for the journey west. Dan and Ben had gone back to the admiral's house, acquiring additional gear for the trip, including a combat helmet and several other attachments for their vests. Ian and Ben had even taken a short trip to a local Army Navy store, finding a couple more pieces of equipment they had deemed necessary for the journey. If asked, Ben not only could act, but absolutely looked the part of a soldier, one that meant some serious business.

While also gearing up, Dan had made a point of setting up a couple of bug out bags for the group, not only for their current trip but for any that may occur in the future. The last couple of days had been relatively quiet, with little to no radio chatter other than check-ins with his group. Roughly an hour before sundown, they would leave. While they all agreed that traveling at night would be dangerous, they also assumed it would keep their movement somewhat hidden from prying eyes.

"I feel a little overprepared for once," Ben said, thinking back on his first trip out of the Sanctuary.

"You could be the most prepared man in the world, and it wouldn't matter. As long as you keep a clear head when the shit hits the fan, you'll be fine," Dan replied as Ben smoothly pulled the flask from his vest, taking a light pull.

The men would take both trucks, leaving Ben's Tesla for Ian and Kelly in case of an emergency. They had even taken the car out of the garage, road testing it all the way to the battery shop. While the vehicle would not fare well off-road, it was more than capable of handling the street.

"I know it's only a two-hour drive to get to where we're going, but last time I had that shit stuck in my head, I stayed out for almost four days, not to mention I wasn't even twenty miles from here," Ben said. He wasn't nervous; however, Ben was apprehensive. Nothing could go wrong on his journey to Sarah. The thought of running into other people didn't bother Ben as much as it had previously. He already had his mind set on the group from Tallahassee being more than welcoming to him. Kelly and Ian had even come up with a few ideas.

Ben's backstory would be simple. He would be from Fort Stewart in Georgia, stopping by Jacksonville on his way west, picking up the truck somewhere along the way. They had even discussed the group in Tallahassee being able to look up records of the state's inhabitants. This level of planning was vital to Ben when he was an actor playing a part.

"So we should expect the first radio check-in at around 7:00 p.m.?" Kelly asked, already knowing the answer. The group had gone through the routine the day prior at nauseam. Ben projected they would be at Lake City pending any significant issues in roughly two hours. The news that the scouts from the capital had been moving freely on Interstate 10 gave them confidence in their timeline.

"Yup. As long as Dan and I are within a quarter-mile of each other, his vehicle's sync system should be able to pick up Eve with the signal extender we tested this morning," Ben said as the mention of the watch's name sprang it to life.

"Good afternoon, Ben. You have an alarm set to go off in thirty minutes. This is also your biweekly reminder that you have four hundred updates pending," Eve chirped again, reminding Ben that he had some figuring out to do when he got back. Ever since their trip to the battery shop, Eve had been reminding him of several updates that had come through the signal from the shop.

This was another one of the items added to the list of things to do in the new world, that kept getting pushed down in its level of importance.

"Eve, silent mode till alarm," Ben instructed, pulling out a small notebook as Ian, Kelly, and Dan circled the trucks parked in the driveway.

"Alright, after pulling out the ammunition for the trip, we're down to five thousand rounds of 5.56mm here. Dan and I are taking two thousand rounds, including five hundred rounds of 9mm ammunition. We're all stocked up on food, and we took enough to touch my stores. I think we're about as ready as we're ever going to be," Ben said to the team standing in front of him.

"Yes, Dad, we'll be good. No parties, no drinking your liquor, and no boys over past midnight," Kelly said, winking at Ian as everybody laughed out loud. Anything to lighten the mood. Ben and Dan were about to set out on a serious trip, which might very well decide their futures.

The two men entered their respective vehicles as Ian opened the front gate. Kelly walked behind them, waving as Ben looked in his rearview mirror, seeing the two with deliberate smiles on their faces. They were keeping it together for the good of the team. In reality, they were as nervous as a pair of dogs that had just eaten their owner's favorite pair of shoes. Ben took a deep breath as his front tires crunched on the road's pavement in front of the turnoff.

Ben and Dan were both familiar with the road up to Interstate 295, making quick time weaving in and out between the abandoned cars. As planned, while the two men's vehicles were close, they could communicate through Eve. Over the past ten years, cars had become communication hubs in their own rights. Wi-Fi boosters, signal enhancers, and near field communication systems were now included in most vehicles, at least before all hell broke loose. Elon Musk had even created a solar truck camper, which was designed to fit almost any truck and had solar panels on top, powering a good portion of the onboard electrical systems. While not enough to power the vehicle into motion, it would allow one to use its electrical systems perpetually.

As the two trucks approached the Buckman Bridge's west side, Ben came over the radio. "I had no idea how bad shit was close to home until I went out that first time and met Ian and Kelly. It looks like the damn D-Day invasion happened here," Ben said, referencing the hundreds of burnt cars. To make the scene even grimmer in the dusky sky before twilight, bones of several hundred skeletons crunched under Ben's tires, clearly once human. The remnants lay strewn on the road, indifferent to whether they'd once belonged to a zombie or a regular person just trying to survive. Ben couldn't believe he'd missed this.

"It's like this in a lot of areas close to bridges," Dan told him, the sound of him flicking a lighter echoing through the stereo system in Ben's truck. "Like your friends back there, I think people just felt like they had to make a stand somewhere, anywhere. A lot of good that got them."

"I guess you're right. It just freaks me out," Ben admitted as Eve started playing Queen's greatest hits lightly through the stereo.

"I'm always right," Dan replied chuckling.

The next forty-five minutes of the drive were as predicted. Two westbound lanes of Interstate 295 had been cleared from the Buckman Bridge through to the Interstate 10 west turnoff. As the sun continued to set, shadows danced along the side of the road. Ben could see all the lumbering figures of zombies wandering on the other side of the piled-up vehicles.

As the blanket of night covered the two trucks, Dan pulled

off to the side of the road under a bridge in an area that didn't have any vehicles.

"Should we be stopping?" Ben asked after at least twenty minutes of listening to music. He had actually zoned out for a short amount of time, imagining days long since past driving down dark roads and the interstate at night listening to music.

"Yeah, I want to check this out. When I came through here last time, this place was a mess. Someone cleared it out, and I'm guessing for a good reason," Dan said as both the men turned up the trucks and lights.

Ben sat there in the dark truck, talking under his breath. "Let's check it out. Let's split up. I have a good idea. Let's go down that dark hallway."

Ben stepped out of the truck with his rifle facing the opposite side of the interstate. The additional gear he had on gave him an extra level of confidence. Dan motioned Ben over.

"You know this area?" Dan whispered, looking around, his eyes shining in the moonlight.

"No. The only thing around here is . . . wait, yeah, there is a grocery distribution center here," Ben said, taking a breath of the humid fall Florida air.

"We need to get mov—" Dan said as a group of zombies tumbled down the hill on the side of the overpass.

The two men paused, watching the goofy pile of zombies. Ben raised his rifle, contemplating if he should release a flurry of death on the already dead.

Shaking his head, Ben took a breath, focusing. "We need to leave now."

Without hesitation, the two men shuffled to their trucks only to see another wave of zombies tumbling down the hill. The slowly moving bodies smacked into the sides of the truck with thuds, followed by slow scraping clear in the quiet night air.

"Shit," Ben whispered as the truck sprang to life. Dan doing so at the same time.

Eve came over the radio as Ben started sweating, working to figure out if he should hold his rifle or the steering wheel as more bodies tumbled down the embankment, slamming hard into the truck. The now growing mass of bodies was rocking the vehicle.

Dan came over the stereo. "Pull forward slowly, don't rush it."

Ben slowly moved the truck forward, the sounds of bodies sliding off the vehicle and into the concrete, making him wince. No fewer than fifty zombies had fallen down the hill, and Ben watched as Dan's truck ran over a few of them, gore exploding as Dan's truck's right side tilted upward, obviously rolling over the initial pile of zombies. Ben's truck also began to do the same. He didn't panic, slowly easing the vehicle further to the left onto the open road.

After what seemed like an eternity, the two trucks were back on the cleared road, driving at fifty miles per hour. "You're not allowed to call the next piss break," Ben said over the radio, giving Dan a hard time. Unlike his usual quick banter, Dan paused, knowing he had made a bad call.

"Yeah, last time, man," was all Dan replied.

After another few minutes of driving, Eve chirped over both of the men's radios, "You have now arrived to the transmission zone."

Instead of coming to a complete stop, Dan slowed the vehicles down to a steady 20 mph.

"Switch channels. I'll call the Sanctuary; you may contact your team. I'll leave the main channel with Eve open," Ben said as he picked up the handheld radio. The sounds of Dan doing the same came through Eve as he heard him calling his friends on the other side. Ben turned up the radio a few notches to make the conversation background noise.

"Sanctuary One, this is B1, over," Ben said flatly.

"This is Sanctuary One. Read you loud and clear, how's it

going?" Kelly's voice came over the radio.

"Only one shitstorm so far. Other than that, just as projected," Ben replied, hearing Ian giggling in the background.

"We only have one shitstorm here," Kelly drawled out, obviously referring to Ian.

"That's a good copy. I met the first marker," Ben said, letting Ian and Kelly know that he would not be on the radio until they reached Dan's team.

"Roger, read you loud and clear," Kelly replied before Ian rustled the radio from her.

"Hey, man, be safe," Ian said, genuinely concerned. They disconnected after that.

After a few minutes of silence and driving slowly, Dan chirped back over the truck stereo system. "Everything good back home?" Dan asked. The comment made Ben smile.

"You called it home, jackass," Ben said as he heard Dan chuckling lightly.

"I guess I did. Everything looks to be clear. Tina is going to meet us before we get to the off-ramp. I told her about our little experience. If you're good, I'm going to put the pedal to the metal and get the hell out of here," Dan said as his truck accelerated.

The one thing Ben had ignored for the majority of the trip was Dan's snowplow on the front of his vehicle, which was now sending several random zombie parts flying to either side of the road, several even hitting Ben's truck.

CHAPTER 15

"That's her," Dan said proudly as a small red light flashed on the side of the road. Without the ambient light of civilization, the world was pitch-black at night. The effect, while chilling, was also calming. The stars and moon in the sky, when clear, gave the night a few extra shades of light, and tonight just happened to be one of those nights.

If it weren't for the lights on the instrument panels inside the truck, Ben would be able to see clearly. They had been driving with their running lights on. While this helped keep their movement silhouetted, it did little to help the two men's night vision.

By then, Ben had transitioned over to the same radio frequency as Dan and his group. "I see you. Follow me," Tina came over the radio. Her voice was smooth yet sharp. After hearing stories of her husband, Dustin, Ben assumed that Tina was a serious woman.

After another fifteen minutes of driving down a two-lane road, Tina in the lead vehicle pulled to the right, leading the caravan down a tree-covered lane. They were clearly out in the country. Ben always thought it humorous when people who lived outside of Florida didn't believe there was a sizable amount of countryside.

After a couple more minutes of driving up what was now a mix of gravel and sand, a light appeared directly in front of them. As the two vehicles stopped, Ben scanned the tree line for movement. By the looks of everything, they were tucked away out of eye or earshot of others.

The sound of car doors opening and closing came muffled from outside Ben's truck. He sat there for a few seconds, taking in the two women hugging Dan. "Eve, put the truck in battery saving mode and set the alarm," Ben instructed, ensuring that if anybody were to touch his truck while he was not looking, they would be in for a surprise.

Dan, Shelly, and Tina walked up to Ben's truck as he stepped out. Ben immediately noticed that Dan had left his weapon in his truck. By the looks of Tina and Shelly, it was clear why. The two women were well-armed, both carrying assault rifles slung over the front of their bodies and pistols hanging from their hips. Both wore dark fatigues, much like Ben's, and they had clearly been out in the shit for some time.

"Ben, nice to meet you. Kinda glad you found the slug wandering around and got him back home," Shelly said, the smile lighting up her face reaching her eyes.

"I've heard a fair amount about the two of you. A pleasure to finely meet you," Ben said sheepishly.

"Yeah, I'm not going to wait any longer. Let's get inside; I want to hear everything," Tina said with a curt smile, walking toward the house.

"She's fine. This is just the first time we've heard anything about Dustin. We're both excited," Shelly reassured, putting her arm around Dan as the two kissed lightly.

After a few minutes of unloading their critical gear and bug out bags, Ben and Dan walked into the house. The building was eclectic and old, lending itself to years of memories long since gone. The easiest way to describe the house in Ben's mind was a log cabin on a small lake. Wood-paneled walls and large timbers overhead gave the house a rustic feel. To finish it off, stone flooring and sizeable country furniture filled the space. The fireplace lit the room at the far end as several electric lights that obviously charged during daytime handled the rest. All the windows were open, letting a cool breeze in as the smell of the pond behind the house filled the air.

"Home sweet home," Dan said as Shelly handed him a drink she had clearly made for him before they pulled up. Ben liked these people immediately.

"You look familiar," Tina said, squinting her eyes in the dull light.

"Yeah, I get that a lot," Ben replied, getting used to people recognizing him during the apocalypse.

"This is the one and only Agent Davenport from the movies. Oh, and by the way, that thing the news said he did? He didn't," Dan clarified, downing his drink in one pull.

"Holy shit. My husband is, like, an awkwardly creepy fan of yours," Tina said, shaking her head. "Anyway, spill it before I lose my shit."

Tina liked to cuss, and did so frequently. It wasn't the kind of language that offended people, but the type that was perfectly timed. The right curse word, used at the right time, was always in fashion in the correct context.

Ben and Dan spent the next hour, telling the two women as much as they could. Ben even went as far as to tell the story of how he met Ian and Kelly. However, the best part of the story was when Ben and Ian had gotten the drop on Dan while he was getting beer out of the gas station. Shelly, after the telling of that heroic tale, was only down to one-word responses. "Typical . . ." As the conversation grew more serious, so did the expressions on the two women's faces.

The gravity of what Ben was there to do and the fact that Dustin was probably still alive was almost too much for the women to bear. Shelly and Tina drank three bottles of wine over the next two hours.

"My God. This is just . . ." Tina trailed off. Shelly was shaken by Ben's resolve to get his wife. It reminded her of Dan's.

"Well, you're either going to get the Husband of the Year

award, or you'll be dead," Tina joked, bringing levity back into the conversation.

"I'd prefer the first," Ben said, letting out a sigh. "I think Sarah would have liked to know you two before all this. I don't plan on being gone long. I'm sure Dan will fill you in when I leave. I think you will like the Sanctuary."

"Hell, anything that gets me closer to Dustin, I'm in. No need to convince me there, movie star. Plus, I'm pretty sure you two wouldn't have hung out with us prior to all this, so save it," Tina said, winking to the group before standing up.

"Where you going?" Dan asked as she walked over, grabbing her backpack and rifle.

"Someone's got to keep your asses safe at night," Tina replied, walking out. In truth, seeing Dan and meeting Ben had her mind on overdrive. She wouldn't be able to sleep.

Shelly, seeing her friend walk out, looked over at Ben. "So, was Dan smoking?"

Ben stuttered, answering her question without talking.

"I knew it. That truck smelled like an ashtray. You, mister, are sleeping on the couch. Well, maybe after tonight," Shelly corrected as the two started laughing.

Ben found himself joining them, finally clearing his throat. "Uhm . . . so tell me your thoughts about the interstate from here to Tallahassee. I already heard Dan's take on things."

Shelly sat up straight. "He tell you how much it sucks?" The expression on Ben's face didn't waver. "Let me guess. He didn't tell you about the body pits," Shelly answered her own question.

"I forgot about those," Dan said, grimacing.

"About forty miles west of here, there's a no-man's-land of bodies and bones. It's not only where the capital's team made a final stand, but it's also where they dump the bodies," Shelly said, leaning back.

"Why not in the ocean?" Ben asked, making a good point.

"From what we can tell, they use it as a deterrent. Shit," Dan said, shaking his head, "If it weren't for her, I'd have had you driving into a shitshow. I'll draw a map. You have to take a short detour. The interstate's blocked for about a quarter of a mile."

"There's a quarter of a mile of bones and rotting zombies?" Ben repeated to himself incredulously.

Realizing that Ben had been sheltered until recently, Dan made sure to bring him back to Earth. "There were, what? Between 300 and 500 million people in the United States when this happened? You've run into what? Eight?" Dan said as the mood shifted. Thoughts of old friends and family showed on the three's faces.

Taking a deep breath, Ben shook his head. "Way to bring the mood down, Dan," Ben said jokingly. "I'm going to get some rest and head out first thing."

As Ben walked off, he could overhear Dan and Shelly talking.

"I like him," Dan said.

"Me too. I don't know why, but I just feel like things are going to work out. Let's make sure he has his story straight one more time in the morning."

"I don't think that's going to be an issue," Dan replied, giving Ben a much-needed boost.

CHAPTER 16

"You smell that?" Ben asked, looking into the hazy sky. "Smells like a fire. I radioed Tina; she's a few miles west checking things out before you leave. Nothing looked off to her," Dan said, walking a five-gallon jug of water to the back of Ben's truck. While supplying enough water to drink, the local spring was hard to work without a functioning pump.

"What's this for?" Ben asked as Dan also handed him a few straps.

"If you run into any fire or have to drive through it, just strap the damn water jug onto your hood. Stab it a bunch of times with your knife—not the Rambo one—and hit the gas," Dan said. The simplicity of the idea made some childish sense to the two men.

"Alright, playtime's over, boys. Ben, you good?" Shelly asked as Dan did a final check on the radio with Tina, letting her know Ben would be leaving soon.

"Everything's good on my end. Dan, I'll do my final radio check about five miles out of the city. If I see anyone, I'll let you know, then wipe the radio." This was all part of the plan. Tina would shadow Ben for several miles, transferring any necessary messages. Once they reached a certain point, she would post up in an area identified on the map. This would be the rally point for Sarah and Ben. Tina, from there, would escort them back. Shelly and Dan would have the job of packing up the house while Ben was away. The plan was to take no longer than five days.

After saying their goodbyes, Ben started the truck, pulling away from the farmhouse. "Eve, play Nine Inch Nails," Ben requested, needing to get focused.

"It's been a while since you last played Nine Inch Nails. Reminder: I will be on silent mode in two hours. I hope I don't miss anything fun," Eve chirped to Ben's surprise.

"What the hell does that mean?" he mumbled, shaking his head.

"Ben, this is Tina, over," the faint staticky voice came over the radio, interrupting Ben's attempt to listen to music.

"Go ahead," Ben said, starting to notice the smokey haze beginning to grow thicker.

"I'm pretty sure you see what I'm seeing by now. I'm not sure how big that fire is, but the winds are blowing to the east, so it's coming from the direction you're heading in. If it gets much thicker, it might be in our best interest to take a break," Tina said as Ben leaned forward, looking up into the sky into his north and south. Getting an unpleasant odor through the truck's vents, Ben flipped the switch to circulate the vehicle's interior air.

Since leaving the farmhouse, Ben had been driving at a steady 20 mph. Including the detour around what they were calling the deadline, the trip should take at least two and a half to three hours. As the miles went by, the smoke grew thicker. Ashes drifted past the windshield, some landing and sticking to the hood of the truck. This didn't break Ben's determination. He was getting there today, come hell or high water.

"Can you smell that, over?" Tina came over the radio again, cutting Ben's music in half.

"Yeah, it stinks. I've got a bad feeling that deadline of yours might be on fire. How much further till we reach the detour, over?" Ben asked, the mental image of lumbering zombies staggering toward him, bringing certain death, forming in his mind.

"Another five damn miles. I think we are on the same page.

Let's get to the turnoff, then figure it out from there. I already radioed the others," Tina said as they continued to drive through the thickening smoke. The worry of fire or not seeing something coming at them had slowed the two down drastically.

After another twenty minutes, the smoke was still thick. While it wasn't getting worse, it wasn't improving either. Ben followed Tina as she cut through a small field, meeting an adjoining road. The detour was clearly not on the map or on a regular exit. After a few more minutes of distancing themselves from the interstate, Tina pulled off the road and into a covered driveway.

She radioed Ben to stop his vehicle and get out. For now, the trip would be delayed, since the possibility of fire covering the detour needed to be discussed. In reality, her main concern was the possibility of scouts from the capital running the back roads.

The house was a safe house the group had scouted and used in the past. Tina pulled out a key and slowly opened the door, the barrel of her shotgun leading the way. Ben grabbed his bag and rifle, following close behind. The sky started turning a red hue as the smoke muffled the sun.

The double-wide trailer sat a mile off a two-lane road a few miles off the interstate. One would have to be looking for the place to find it, and even then, with all the other options, this place would not register on the list of places to go.

As the two walked into the house, Tina flipped on a handful of LED lights, lowering the mask from her face and taking a breath. While the smell of smoke lingered in the air, it had not permeated through the walls yet.

"One of your safe houses?" Ben asked, sitting on the large brown recliner.

"My uncle used to live here. It's the secondary site we mentioned using in case there was an issue with the other. By the looks of the smoke, this is now the primary location," Tina replied, grabbing a bottle of wine off the counter.

"I was about to say there's no way anyone would find this

place," Ben said, pulling out his flask as well, getting a calming drink.

"You mean 'cause it's a shithole? That's okay, it is." She peeked through the blinds in the kitchen window overlooking the front yard. Woods surrounded the trailer, shading the house for the majority of the day. Cheap shag carpet and laminate paneling topped off the home.

Ben squinted his eyes, thinking about one of the preppers shows he had watched. "Since we don't know where this fire's coming from, I think I'm going to stick around till night."

Tina looked at Ben with a confused expression.

Taking another long pull of spiced rum, Ben wiped his lips. It was before noon, but the day drinking law was in effect. "At night, you can see the fire. It will glow like city lights," Ben said, sounding smarter than he was about the topic.

Tina, impressed by his knowledge, raised her glass in salute. "Zombies, smoke, and fire. What could go wrong," she joked as the two sat in the living room, finishing off their beverages.

Ben grabbed another bottle to calm his nerves. The rest of the day consisted of dry conversation and patience running out. As if the apocalypse gods knew this, several thumps on the side of the house, made the two inhabitants jump.

"Expecting company?" Ben said sarcastically as the joke went flat.

The two quickly grabbed their weapons, leaning against the living room wall. Tina put her ear to the paneling, the thin walls allowing her to hear what was happening on the other side.

"Two, maybe three zombies. They might just keep going," Tina said, as Ben shook his head, pointing at the silencer at the end of this rifle. She nodded. The change of pace was actually a welcome distraction. Ben walked out the front door as Tina held it open before following behind, picking up the baseball bat she had brought with her.

As they turned the corner of the house, three pitch-black,

charred zombies slowly shuffled in their direction, taking the two by surprise. The skin on the zombies' bodies looked like burnt charcoal, and bones peeked out from various areas.

"What the fuck," Ben whispered as Tina let out a huff. The two came to the same conclusion. Wherever these zombies had come from was the source of the fire. The smoke lingering in the air made the woods behind the lumbering bodies fuzzy.

Tina pointed her bat at the straggler as Ben pulled up his rifle, letting out a burst of muffled rounds into the skulls of the other two. *Pat, tat, tat. Pat, tat, tat,* came from the death machine as the charred heads exploded, exposing what Ben could only assume were cooked, rotted zombie brains. The two of them had the same disgusted look on their faces, similar to the face one made when witnessing a person eating something truly disgusting. The smell was too much for either of them to get close enough to check the bodies. Things like wallets were a great way of telling where a zombie was from.

The two walked back in, taking stock of what they had just witnessed.

"That was a new one for me. How about you?" Tina asked as Ben checked the action on his rifle.

"Same. I'm starting to wonder if this is the reason there have been so many patrols lately," Ben said, walking back over to the brown recliner.

"I'm not sure. The smoke just started up. Hell, I'm surprised we haven't run into anyone else. If you're dead set on leaving tonight, It may actually work to your favor if you make it," Tina said, making a good point.

"Yeah, if I make it. I'm going. If it gets too bad, I'll turn around and come back here," he said, starting to refocus on his end goal. He wasn't going to fight a war; he was simply going to walk up and say hello, do some acting, and sneak out with Sarah. After talking with the new group, Ben had a good idea of how to make that happen.

"Want to see something cool?" Tina asked, flashing a wry smile at Ben. He nodded as she walked off into the bedroom at the back of the trailer, leaving him alone in the living room. The sounds of something falling to the floor reverberated through the trailer as Tina came back.

Lying at Ben's feet were a firefighter's respirator, mask, tank, and boots. He looked at Tina, smirking. "Well played."

"My uncle was a firefighter for as long as I can remember. Living out in the country, he spent most of that time in the auxiliary or something like that. I was thinking, if things get too bad, just throw this stuff on," Tina said, looking at the equipment fondly.

"You really liked your uncle, didn't you," Ben said, seeing her face go slack.

She took a deep breath. "I grew up running around these woods. Hell, I learned how to fish in the pond out back. My dad would always bring me here when he and Mom wanted some adult time, as they called it. My uncle would always go out of his way to make sure I had the best time. I did."

"I had something like that growing up, but not as frequent. I used to love going to my grandparent's house. When my grandmother got sick, things changed. Anyway, I'll put this to good use," Ben promised as Tina rubbed her hand across the tank.

"You know, I wish there was a way to go back in time before all this shit, and know we were in the good old days before we left them," Tina said as Ben raised an eyebrow. The phrase sounded familiar.

After an hour of going through the equipment, the reddish sun started to set, the smoke outside remaining at a steady red haze up until dusk. It was time. Checking his equipment once again and picking up the firefighter's gear from Tina's uncle, Ben was ready to go. "Eve, time check," he said, putting Eve back to work.

"It's now 6:30 p.m. According to the designated route, you

have forty miles until you reach your destination. You have five miles to reach Interstate 10. Would you like to hear some light, easy listening?" Eve chirped, letting Ben know that he was, in fact, ignoring her more and more.

"Well, it's been nice knowing you," Tina joked, chuckling. "In all seriousness, be safe. Come back to the group and make sure your wife, Sarah, is with you. Not a lot of good shit happens these days. Let's at least try to get this one win."

Ben didn't say a word, only nodded, turning to the door and walking out into the hazy night. Before leaving, Ben—at Dan's suggestion—strapped the five-gallon watercooler to his vehicle's hood. Starting the truck, he looked back through the mirror at the house. He would come back here, and he would do whatever it took to ensure that happened.

CHAPTER 17

Tallahassee, the day Ben left with Tina

"What's going on?" Nicole asked, sitting in Sarah's office as an extra layer of noise started emanating from the hospital's main lobby.

"I don't know," Sarah replied. John chose that moment to knock, walking through the door.

"You guys have to check this out," he said, motioning the two women to follow him. Several people were shuffling around in different directions as they entered the hospital's lobby.

Sarah had met with the team from New York, giving them a clean bill of health not long after seeing them. While not getting into details, they'd told Sarah an abbreviated version of their story. It was both heroic and tragic at the same time. Chris and the Court would definitely want to keep these people around. Sarah didn't even doubt they would be her neighbors in the tower at some point.

"Where are we going?" Nicole asked John as he kept walking, determined to get to their destination. He didn't want any distractions, needing to get them as high up in the building as they could, which just happened to be the tower in which Sarah lived.

"High ground," was all John replied.

Sarah started getting uneasy, thinking there may be an

issue or some trouble involving their plan. This was soon dispelled by seeing various other people running around in a determined fashion.

The community was buzzing with energy with one common goal: to figure out whatever the hell it was everyone was so worked up about.

The elevator lurched to a stop, dinging as the doors roughly slid open. John motioned the two women to the eastern-facing window on the other side of the building. What lay before their eyes was both concerning and breathtaking. Plumes of smoke and fire rose as far as the eye could see, stretching from north to south. The wind was blowing in the opposite direction, keeping the smoke from invading the city of Tallahassee.

"A fire, and a nasty one. Some scouts just came in and said it went as far north as they dared to travel, almost to the damn gulf. I was talking to Patrick at the front gate—he used to work for Game and Wildlife or something like that—and he said he was surprised that half the damn state hadn't been burned to the ground yet without properly controlled burns," John spit out quickly as Sarah started doing the math in her head.

She started wondering if Ben was causing the fires or if they were somehow a danger to him. Either way, the timing was suspicious at best. Little did she know, Ben was on his way and determined not to stop.

Seeing the look on Sarah's face, John was wondering the same thing. "Is this . . . ?" John started, not finishing his sentence.

"No, I don't think so. Were the scouts able to make it on the interstate?" Sarah asked as her heart skipped a beat.

John took a calming breath. "They said the road was clear all the way to the deadline. Beyond that, they weren't sure." The three of them turned away from the window.

Ben had indeed made it to the deadline and was frantically trying to get back to Interstate 10. The scene laid out in front of the group, pushing doubt into their minds.

While the two women trusted him on the surface, there was still some doubt. On the other hand, John was determined to leave with the group. He wouldn't admit it yet, but he was in love with Nicole. Not the kind of love that went away after a few days, but the type that made you change the way you lived your life. If they made it out of the capital without issue, John planned on telling her just that.

"We should be processing a new person soon," Sarah said nervously, referring to Ben. Nicole and John hadn't witnessed this type of anxiety from Sarah, so the two took note.

"Alright, everybody, get back to what you were doing. I'm going to stay out by the gate today. Keep your radio handy in case I need to call for either one of you. Just switch over to the other channel we discussed earlier. With all this fire, it won't seem irregular for me to be up at the gate," John said, taking whatever control he could of the situation to calm Sarah's nerves. It worked. She shook her head, and the three of them walked back into the elevator.

Walking back into her office, Sarah saw Chris standing there with a stack of folders in his hand. The light from the LED bulbs shone annoyingly on the man's bald head.

"I see you went to look at the fire. Not too many people are allowed on the higher floors of the building. You are one of the few people who should understand the gravity of the situation," Chris said as Sarah nodded in acknowledgment, walking over to her desk and hitting the button on her coffee maker.

"Coffee?" she asked in a normal tone, not letting Chris know she was, in fact, a nervous wreck.

"No, I'm fine. I appreciate it, though. I wish everyone else around here had manners like you," Chris said, walking closer to Sarah, invading her personal space. "I'm going to need you to do me a favor. By now, I'm fairly confident you understand why we have you examine the people that come in here looking for refuge. If I'm right, that fire is going to drive about every single living person between it and the capital directly toward us. When that time comes, things may get a little messy. I'm going to need you to be at your best when people come in. We won't be spending nearly as much time going through their background and medical history as we have been. All I need is a simple yes or no."

Sarah stood there unwavering, picking up her coffee mug out of the single-serve machine. She was a pro, plus she was married to an actor. There wasn't even a ripple on the surface of the cup. Chris looked down, noticing the small detail as Sarah knew he would; she had done that on purpose.

"Then you know my opinion on this," Sarah responded without having to say anything more, deciding to be honest. This wasn't the time to lie.

"That is precisely why you are still here doing your job. If you didn't take issue with any of this, I would be concerned. Look, I don't walk around explaining myself to people or justifying what I do, but you need to understand something: I struggle with this at times as well. That's why we came up with this system. If we had let everyone who came to our gates stay, I'm pretty sure this place would've been overrun and destroyed by now.

"I can tell by the expression on your face that you understand. I'm not a monster, and neither are you. I know you've slipped a few people through recently, and I'm taking it as you having a reason to do so; therefore, they stay. I'm also sure you know that, even if we don't accept somebody into the community, we give them plenty of provisions to get them somewhere," Chris said, explaining everything Sarah already knew.

It was good for her to hear it coming from Chris. She was surprised at the level of knowledge the man had, not only about what she was doing, but about the way she thought. He was right, and as she had mentioned plenty of times before, he wasn't a monster. While on the surface, it may seem that way, she also knew what would happen if they let everybody behind the walls.

Sarah nodded her head in agreement as Chris smiled. "I'll make you a promise as well. We have been talking about expanding the outer perimeter to take on more people. Not the city center, but the outer walls and fences," he clarified. "After this is over, we will bring you into the Court, and we'll discuss how many people we can add. I know it doesn't seem like much, but we need to be ready just in case something like this happens again."

The statement made Sarah happy, the smile on her face genuine, reaching her eyes. It sounded as if the Court was trying to figure out a way to take on more people, and the possibility of that gave her new hope for the community. She would be able to direct people to the capital in the future.

As Chris walked out of the office, a red light flashed in the lobby as an alarm sounded. "Well, that didn't take long," he said, nodding to Sarah before he walked out the door.

CHAPTER 18

Ben pulled out of the covered drive, the smoke immediately thickening around him. He could see roughly ten feet in front of his truck. It was just enough to allow him to maneuver on the roads, however, he didn't like his inability to see any large groups of zombies outside of that small bubble.

"Eve, silent mode, please," Ben requested, needing to concentrate on the road; she had started playing some light music in the background.

"Anything for you," Eve chirped back as Ben jerked up straight, looking around the cab. Over the last two days, Eve had responded with several phrases he hadn't programmed her to say. He would need to take a look at that later. For now, he needed to focus on the task at hand. According to the maps, he was a little under forty miles away from his target, and Sarah.

Embers flickered in front of the headlights as Ben started to sweat lightly. He looked over at the gear Tina had given him, which he had set in the front seat. If the smoke got much thicker, he would have to put it on. A loud thump echoed on the vehicle's side. Ben looked in the rearview mirror only to see a charred zombie smack the ground. He was going around five miles per hour, and any faster just wasn't in the cards.

"Dammit," Ben chuffed under his breath. Another zombie appeared out of the smoke directly in front of the truck, rolling underneath its carriage. The creature's head smacked the hood as black, charred, rotted flesh flaked off, wisping over the windshield.

Another thump from the truck's left backside and a light glow to Ben's front were competing for his attention. This would be the first time he saw anything glowing, telling him that fire was indeed near.

The smoke was making it hard to breathe by now. "Well, Eve, this is it. Either we make it out of this alive, or we're gonna make one hell of a meat pie for these damn zombies." He took down the contents of his recently replenished flask.

Reaching over, Ben grabbed the face mask and oxygen tank, quickly slipping it over his head and releasing the valve as cool, refreshing air started to flow into his nostrils. Ben took a deep, clearing breath. The fresh oxygen washing euphoria through Ben like a drug.

The zen moment was short-lived as two glowing figures emerged from the smoke in front of the truck, forcing him to slam on the brakes. In front of Ben were two honest-to-God flaming zombies, still moving somehow. Embers were dancing off their bodies as gusts of wind pushed the fire's heart and pumped vital life-sustaining blood into it.

The sheer absurdity of what he was witnessing froze Ben in place momentarily. He snapped out of it as Eve, against his commands, chirped to life. "Your heart rate is extremely elevated. I am going to play some calming music for you."

"Creep" by Radiohead came through the speakers as Ben regained his faculties. "Eve, we're going to need to have a chat after this. No full charges for you till we get home," Ben said, making himself laugh. He grabbed the pistol and opened the door.

He wouldn't run over the flaming zombies for fear of catching the truck on fire. The oxygen tank had a strap on it, allowing Ben to throw it over the front of his vest. He could feel the direct heat outside, like opening an oven door. The fire was south of his location; he could see a red, pulsating mass. While it was close, it looked as if he would be able to make it back to the interstate.

The two glowing masses lumbering in front of the truck were attracted by the truck's lights. They were too far gone to look for Ben, so he pulled up his pistol, shooting them both. He assumed he hit their chests, as Ben's mask was starting to fog over; the smoke was too thick to allow him any precise shots. As planned, the two red dots shuffled off the road, seeming to slip over each other and falling on the ground as another small fire started to erupt from the grass.

As Ben turned around to get back in his truck and get the hell out of there, several dozen more red glowing dots started to appear from what Ben assumed was a field to the south. Feeling the day's frustrations, he leaned against the truck, sighted his rifle, and released a barrage of rounds, putting the weapon on fully automatic. It only took a few seconds to expend the ammunition as several thumps from the other side of the truck told Ben his time on that piece of road was over. It was time to go.

Taking a moment, he saw several shadows dancing in the smoke. He turned his attention to the watercooler strapped to the hood and let loose several rounds from his pistol into it, not losing time before jumping into the truck and bringing it to life. He glanced at the map on the readout. It was a straight shot to the interstate from there. Gritting his teeth, Ben floored the truck as a rush of embers and smoke took hold of the windshield. A glowing red dot appeared in front of the truck as Ben slammed into it, crunching the charred zombie on the grill. Water splashed the windscreen; the seemingly stupid trick was working.

The red glow was getting closer on both sides, and the temperature in the truck increased. Still resolute, Ben pushed the truck harder as he let out a guttural scream, "AGGHHHHH!"

As if the gods had been looking out for Ben, after a whoosh and sudden rush of clear night sky, Ben punched through the smoke and fire.

It took him a few seconds to realize what had just happened. As he brought the truck to a halt, he mentally focused on getting his hands to release the steering wheel. He had left several grooves in the padded covering.

Breathing heavily, Ben took stock of his surroundings. The wind was blowing east, making the smoke nonexistent to the west. He had done it. The road ahead was clear. The interstate 10 turnoff lay directly in front of him.

Stepping out of the truck, Ben grabbed his rifle, sliding the oxygen mask off. A cool, refreshing breeze blew on his face as he took another deep breath. Ben was wearing his full military outfit—including a vest and helmet. His uniform was completely soaked with sweat, making the breeze feel slightly cook on his skin. Turning around, Ben looked at his truck. The once pristine vehicle was now charred and showing its toughness.

The plastic on the doors and rearview mirrors were weathered and partially melted. The stickers and decals that had been on the truck were also fading or gone, showing the only clean part of the truck left. The five-gallon water jug had shaken loose from the vehicle's hood at some point, leaving a dent on it. As Ben walked around the front, it was clear how close he had come to not making it. The plastic molded bumper had melted entirely, and a couple of charred zombie parts sat lodged into the grill. Smoke still rose from the carcasses as he pulled out his big knife, scraping them off.

Turning toward the fire, Ben could see hundreds of zombies lumbering out of the smoke. They looked like nightmare fuel. Half of them were on fire, as the flames and smoke silhouetted the other half.

In typical Ben fashion, he cracked a joke as he reached down and realized his flask was empty. "Too bad they can't make a truck commercial about this shit. I'd buy the hell out of it."

Laughing to himself, Ben jumped back in, taking off into the night.

EPILOGUE

Headlights beamed at the gate set up at the second exit off Interstate 10 labeled "Tallahassee." The vehicle's engine stopped, but the driver left the lights on, covering his figure as he stepped out.

"You need to turn those lights off and step back, please," one of the guards shouted over a megaphone.

The figure raised his hand, clicking the vehicle's remote and turning the lights off. Having bought a few seconds to size up the people managing the gate, the driver walked forward confidently. John squinted at the hulking figure in fatigues.

The guard with the megaphone turned back, shrugging his shoulders. The look of the man in front of them intimidated the group. John was, for all intents and purposes, the current highest-ranking member present. While not in charge of the gate, it was clear the others were turning to him for guidance.

Taking a deep breath, John walked over to the thin man holding the megaphone. "I'm going to need you to drop your weapons and hang tight for a few minutes," John said as he pointed at the woman in the tower. He was starting to question the level of expertise of the people Chris had put on the gates, as the guard still hadn't put the spotlight on the figure. After a second of fiddling with the overly aggressive light, it finally blasted their new guest, forcing him to shield his eyes. The guard dimmed the light slightly, finally getting in step.

The man held his hands up, pulling a pistol from his vest and a large knife from his waist. He placed both items on the ground before standing back up.

John's mind was on overdrive. There was no way the man standing in front of them was Ben. He was, by any measure, a beast. He was large, muscular, and armed to the teeth in military-grade gear, with—what John assumed was—a truck full of weapons.

John hadn't noticed the vehicle initially, only enough to point his finger at it as the woman in the tower blasted the light at the brutalized truck. "Jesus Christ," John mumbled under his breath now. The sight was horrific. Chunks of burnt zombies still clung to what was left of the melted bumper and grill.

"Did you just drive through the fire?" John asked, starting to think this might just be Ben. It was only his aggressive appearance that made John doubt himself.

"Yup," was all Ben replied as he took a breath.

"What's your name? Where are you from?" John continued to ask, only to realize Ben wouldn't be using his real identity. Sarah had told him as much.

"I'm Billy, from Georgia. Do you mind if I keep on trucking west? I just saw some lights and decided to stop. I'm not looking for any trouble," Ben said, already starting to play the part.

You could hear the group behind them let out a collective breath. Ben was intimidating, and the team assigned to the gate that night was less than the Court's A-team. Chris had put his more experienced teams to the south of town, figuring most people were staying in the coastal areas. He was, of course, right in his assumption.

"Not going to be possible tonight. Plus, the interstate is blocked off a few miles up the road," John said as he walked out, opening the gate. The sound of several gunshots echoed in the night air, getting everyone's attention. John's radio jumped to life.

"There's a group of twenty to thirty Zs at gate four. We

got them in one of the ditches," the voice came over the small speaker. That's what the group called large holes dug into the ground. It was a way to conserve ammunition. They would shoot a few zombies to lead them into a ditch, then burn them.

"You guys need a hand?" Ben asked grinning.

"I think we've got it," John replied, keying up his radio still standing in front of Ben. "I have a white male, mid-to-late thirties. I'm guessing military, by the looks of him," he said over the radio.

"Clear to bring in," a bored voice came back.

"Well, it looks like you have a place to stay tonight if you want. We're going to need to keep this truck here till morning, if you're good with that. You can ride in with me. Get yourself checked out by the doc and figure it out from there. If you want to leave, you can. I will just need to escort you through to the far gate," John explained, taking a closer look at the man. He knew what Ben looked like, being a fan of Agent Davenport.

It became clear to John as he came closer to shake the man's hand that it was indeed Ben. Sarah hadn't mentioned the several layers of muscle he had gained since his last movie. Ben noticed the slight change of expression on John's face. It was one of recognition, followed by the immediate burying of the knowledge.

"Sounds good to me. I could use some rest after tonight. Plus, I'm pretty sure I need to get my truck checked out. Anyone around that can do that?" Ben asked, confused by the vibe the man was giving off.

"We can do that," John replied, motioning to the guards to open the gate fully. After a few minutes, Ben had pulled his truck through the gate and cross-loaded a few things. John made sure to put Ben's weapons in the back of his vehicle. As the two men jumped into the Jeep Wrangler, John radioed ahead, letting them know they were coming. He immediately followed that by turning the radio off entirely.

"Ben, I'm a friend of Sarah's. We need to talk . . ." he started as the Jeep rocketed toward the city.

***

"Did you hear that?" Kelly asked, sitting up in a sun lounger behind Ben's house. She was in a bikini getting a tan while drinking a glass of chilled white wine.

Ben and Dan had left the day before, and the two young lovers had planned on taking some time to relax.

Ian leaned over, stretching. The book on his chest creating a large white patch on his now mostly sunburned skin. "Whaa . . ." Ian exclaimed, still waking up.

"Shhh . . ." Kelly whispered as the sound of several thumps came from the front of the house. Ian sat up straight, finally hearing the same thing.

The two jumped up from what they had deemed their honeymoon, running toward the house, grabbing their rifles. The two looked ridiculous in their swimwear with rifles slung over their fronts.

"Is that coming from the gate?" Ian asked, as Kelly scanned the perimeter wall.

"It sounds like it is . . . I can't really tell," Kelly replied, faltering.

Ian pointed at the top of Ben's house. "We can see over the wall from there," he reminded Kelly, as the two bolted back inside the house, securing the door behind them.

After a few moments climbing stairs, the two stood on Ben's roof, looking over the wall. What they saw stunned them. Several hundred zombies scattered in random groups swarmed the woods like ants on an anthill, the indiscriminate movement making it hard to focus on just one of them.

The two looked at each other, wondering what their next move should be.

Acknowledgments

Special thanks go out to all my family, friends, and
the authors that still inspire me to do more.

Jarret LeMaster, thanks for bringing a voice to this series.

To my family, my wife and two sons. This book is part of my
legacy to you. When I am but a memory in time, you will always
be able to pick this book up and remember what a nerd I really
am, was, and, well ... still am ...plus will be some more.

P.S. Hey, Netflix, tick tock...

www.justinleslie.com
Facebook Justin Leslie
Buy Max Abaddon and the Will - Book 1
Buy Max Abaddon and the Purity Law - Book 2

www.ingramcontent.com/pod-product-compliance
Lightning Source LLC
Chambersburg PA
CBHW032156190626
46808CB00021B/1182